SUGAR PORT

SUGAR DADDIES #11

CHARITY PARKERSON

--Warning: This book is intended for readers over the age of 18.

Copyright © 2019 Charity Parkerson
Editor: Vicky Reese and Consultants
Cover designed by: Golden Czermak
ISBN: 978-1-946099-47-1
All rights reserved.

INTRODUCTION

KATO DOESN'T REALIZE HE NEEDS A PORT. UNTIL
BRAD STORMS IN, THAT IS.

Meeting Brad is a soothing balm to Kato's soul. Since
he lost his eyesight two years ago, nothing has been
the same. Where he'd once been chased by all the
men, now he feels like he's nothing more than a
burden on the only friend he has left. Then, Brad
bursts into his life.

It's been a year since Brad caught his ex
cheating. Losing their seven-year relationship under
such ugly circumstances has left Brad slightly bitter.
He's definitely less trusting than before. That's why,
when a sexy and much younger man catches his eye,
Brad is determined to keep his heart out of the deal.

Two jaded men find common ground in the most
unexpected way. But someone will have to be the

first to take a chance on love if they hope to be more than a nighttime fling.

ONE

Valentine's Day at the Den of Payne was every bit as ridiculous as Brad feared it would be. Nude men in nothing but angel wings and looking like twink Cupids. Bad music. Drinks with God only knew what in them. The sounds of sex and fake laughter surrounded him. Brad found an empty loveseat in the center of the room and sat. Even though the scenery at the exclusive sex club was horrid, it was better than being alone, especially tonight. Valentine's Day sucked for single people. For Brad, this day was twice the torment. This day on the calendar marked a year since he'd left early from his job working as Jude and John Green's lawyer at Green's Fighter Fuel to get home before his longtime live-in boyfriend. He'd planned to go all out decorating so everything would be perfect when he proposed. Instead, he'd found Easton face down and ass up, getting plowed by a guy Easton had made Brad believe was Easton's cousin. The dude had been staying with them. He was "family" who'd fallen on hard times. It turned out the only hard times around their house were the ones Rob had been giving Easton under the roof Brad paid for every month for the past seven years. Yeah. Valentine's Day was bullshit. Brad didn't want to go home to an empty house. It was empty in the literal sense as well since Brad hadn't wanted any of the furniture Easton had probably fucked everyone else on. All Brad owned now was a new bedroom suit, a couch and a TV. He wasn't bitter. Much.

Brad tore his thoughts away from the bleak place they'd lingered on all day and focused on the closest naked angel. He was pretty and young. Everyone looked young since Brad turned forty. He was too old for this shit, but his friend Detroit had slipped him a free two-day pass and here Brad was, sulking. Detroit's husband owned this club and people fought to get whipped by him. Brad wondered many times how Detroit stood knowing Payne ran a BDSM club. It was possible catching Easton cheating had left him scarred and overly jealous. Still, he wasn't sure he could handle knowing the man he loved worked in a sex club.

"It's ridiculous, isn't it?"

Brad's head whipped around as the spot beside him became suddenly occupied. A man who looked to be in his early twenties plopped down on the couch. His wide shoulders took up too much space. Brad couldn't look away. The guy's Oxford style shirt, rolled up to the elbows, had his perfectly chiseled forearms on display. Then the guy turned his head. Dark blue eyes captured Brad's focus. Brad's gaze refused to budge.

"I'm sorry?"

The guy motioned toward their surroundings. "This place in full Cupid mode, it's ridiculous, but it's better than sitting home alone. I'm Kato," he said holding out his hand. "Kato Benita."

Brad accepted his handshake. "Brad Hollister."

The sexiest sounding chuckle Brad had ever heard caressed his ears. It was accompanied by an amazing smile. "Sounds like a lawyer's name."

A surprised laugh escaped Brad. "That was a hell of a guess."

Kato's eyebrows rose. Humor filled his expression. "You're not really a lawyer, are you?"

Brad couldn't stop shaking his head in his

surprise. "I am. I work exclusively for Jude and John Green at Green's Fighter Fuel."

"That sounds like an amazing gig."

Kato looked... nice. Way too nice to be hanging out in a sex club. Brad suddenly felt the need to explain why he was there. "My friend, Detroit, he gave me a two-day pass to check out the place. I thought, what the hell. Like you said, it's better than being alone."

"You're friends with Detroit?"

Brad nodded. "In passing. Through a friend of a friend. I take it you know him too."

The gorgeous bright smile was back. "We went to high school together." That definitely put Kato in his early twenties. Damn. Brad seemed to have a knack for finding the youngest man in the room. Kato's gaze never wavered from Brad. It was as if they were in a cafe and nothing sexual happened around them. Brad's interest grew.

"Are you enjoying this, or can I convince you to have dinner with me instead?"

"Dinner with you sounds like a fantastic idea, but I can't leave. I'm on the clock."

Against his will, Brad's eyebrows hit his hairline. Horror overcame him. "Oh. I'm sorry. I didn't realize you were working. Do I owe you a tip or something?

This is my first time in a place like this. I don't know how it works." The more he spoke, the more luminous Kato's smile became until it turned into a chuckle. He didn't bother hiding his humor over Brad's discomfort.

"I answer the phones and give membership tours. Things like that. I work in the office," Kato explained, his voice heavy with laughter. "I'm just on my break."

Brad was horrified on every level. This wasn't going well. He'd basically accused Kato of being for sale. Brad was so damn far out of his comfort zone in this place. No matter how hard he tried to relax, he couldn't. "I'm so sorry. You said you work here, and I don't know what I pictured." Brad's shoulders fell. "I'm sorry."

Kato's smile fell. "Stop apologizing." Brad's teeth immediately snapped closed. He couldn't explain the reaction. It was as if his body awaited Kato's command. "Ask me to dinner for tomorrow night."

A vibration ran through Brad. His gaze wouldn't budge from Kato's hardened expression. His words had the bite of a dare—like Kato challenged Brad to take him on. "May I take you to dinner tomorrow night?"

"Text me your number and I'll send you my address."

Brad dug out his phone while Kato rattled off his number. He texted Kato immediately, so Kato could save his number. Kato's phone repeated everything back as it came through. He'd never heard anyone's phone do that. Maybe when he wasn't so nervous, he'd ask Kato which app he used, because that was a feature he could use for work. Right now, though, he thought it best if he made himself scarce. This place wasn't to his tastes, except for Kato's presence.

A brief smile passed over Kato's lips. "And now you're ready to make a run for it."

Brad shook his head. "You're easily the most intuitive person I've ever met." His gaze swept over Kato's features once more. The dark hair covering Kato's jaw made Brad's hands itch to touch it. "I imagine you'll have to get back to work soon, and I'm not sure this place is for me."

"Oh, I don't know," Kato said, sounding thoughtful. "You've only seen the public viewing stuff. There's a lot that goes down in private around here that might interest you. Maybe I'll convince you to let me show you someday."

Someday? Hell. Brad would let Kato show him whatever he wanted in private right now. Nothing good came of rushing things though. "Maybe so," Brad said instead, deciding to go with the safe response. He stood. "I'll keep an eye out for your text and we'll figure out a time for tomorrow night. It's been nice meeting you."

Kato held his hand out again. This time, when Brad placed his hand in Kato's, Kato tugged him closer and touched his lips to the back of Brad's hand. Brad blushed and looked away. He had no idea what it was about Kato that left him feeling like a bumbling mess. Brad couldn't stop.

"Agreed. It's been the best night I've had in ages."

Brad's blush deepened at Kato's claim. With a final dip of his chin, Brad headed for the door. He didn't notice a single detail even as he passed several blatant sexual acts. His brain was too busy plotting his next move. Next time he saw Kato, Brad would do his damnedest to leave Kato floored.

A SMILE HOVERED on Kato's lips. The scent of expensive cologne still lingered from Brad's presence. Kato fought the urge to chase him. It had been a while since anyone captured his attention. It had been even longer since he'd been excited about anything. Brad Hollister had managed to elicit both reactions in less than an hour. He had Kato's attention.

Kato dug out his phone and felt for the button. He brought the device to his lips. "Save latest text under new contact, Brad."

"Brad saved."

Detroit appeared over Kato's shoulder, startling him. "I still have yet to figure out how you always manage to find the hottest person in the room even without your sight."

A smile stretched Kato's lips at the sound of Detroit's voice. He missed his friend's face. "I follow the smell. Sexy has a certain scent." He leaned closer to Detroit and inhaled. "You smell taken," he said with a laugh, leaning away. "What did he look like anyhow?"

Detroit dropped down onto the couch beside him, making the furniture bounce beneath his weight. He shifted closer until their thighs touched. It was one of Detroit's best qualities that he always knew exactly what Kato needed. He missed human contact. No one touched him anymore.

After draping his arm across the back of the couch behind Kato, Detroit painted him an image.

"Six-two. Trim. Supermodel style to match his beauty. Full, pouty lips. His eyes are truly amazing. They are green but super light. I'm trying to think of something to compare them to, so you can picture them. Oh, I know," Detroit said, snapping his fingers. "Do you remember our sophomore year when, during playoffs, they put us up in that seedy hotel overnight?"

Kato's smile brightened. "How could I forget? We slipped out after everyone else fell asleep and ran across the street to that hole-in-the-wall bar."

Detroit chuckled. Kato heard the smile in his voice. "We fully expected to get thrown out on our asses, but that hot girl was working the bar. She took one look at you and was immediately willing to give us whatever."

"I'm pretty sure it was you she had her eye on," Kato said, interrupting.

"Whatever. Anyhow," Detroit said, sounding put out. "Do you remember those horrible mint drinks they had?"

"Um, yeah. I'm pretty sure we almost died."

Detroit laughed harder. "Yep. That's the only other time I've seen anything the same unnatural green as Brad's eyes."

Kato nodded. Those had been some disgusting

drinks, but they'd looked delicious. Damn, he missed his vision sometimes. "And his hair?"

"Dark brown. Almost black," Detroit answered. Kato could hear how sexy Brad was by listening to the timber of Detroit's voice.

"I don't think he realized I'm blind. If so, he didn't let on."

Detroit somehow managed to shift even closer. Kato appreciated the comfort. "You're good at hiding it, but I don't think Brad is the type to care. Honestly, I'm not sure why he accepted the visitor's pass I gave him."

Kato got it. Brad was lonely. If anyone could recognize longing in others, it was Kato. He felt alone most of the time. Being literally trapped in the dark made loneliness cut so much deeper. "Chances are good I'll never hear from him again, but he seemed nice. I guess I should get back to work."

"There's no hurry." Detroit moved closer and dropped his voice. "Flynn is watching you. He's leaned against the bar, staring like his skin is on fire. He's not bad, you know. I know how you like them older and experienced. He's in his early forties. Easily six-four. Dark red hair. So dark it's almost brown. Sky-blue eyes. A hint of freckles across his nose. In truth, he looks a tad angelic for such a hardcore dom. We get tons of requests for his services as you know."

Kato tried keeping his voice level. He didn't want to give away his distaste. "He's made his interest known. To be honest, I'm not sure he hasn't fetishized me." It wasn't unusual for that to happen, which was something Kato hadn't realized until he'd lost his sight two years ago.

A hint of concern filled Detroit's tone. "I hadn't thought of that. Would you like me to keep him away from you?"

A smile exploded across Kato's face. He loved Detroit. "That's sweet." Of course, Detroit hadn't thought of anyone wanting Kato only because he was blind. Detroit was a good person. "I can still take care of myself." He shrugged. "Who knows? Maybe one night I'll be overcome with the sudden desire to be a helpless mess of a man who can't live without his domination."

Detroit's chuckle warmed Kato's heart. "Yeah. You're right. I can't picture that."

"Incoming text from Brad."

Another sexy laugh sounded from Detroit's side of the couch. "I'll let you run away to your office now, so you can sext with your new hottie."

Kato pushed from the couch. "Thanks for that.

You should go find that husband of yours and beg for a spanking, you lucky bastard." Even Kato heard the laughter in his voice. He didn't wait around for a goodbye. Kato wished he could move fast, but he was still learning to navigate the shadows. He could make out the outline of people in certain lighting, but the Den of Payne was too dark. He had to rely heavily on his other senses and memory. Luckily, people here liked to be touched. If he accidentally brushed someone, they usually chalked it up to being part of the experience.

The air changed, signaling he was close to his office. The playroom was stifling and packed with body heat. The office area was mostly empty and cooler. Kato felt a weight lifting from his shoulders the closer he got to being alone.

A solid arm slid across his lower back. Kato suppressed an irritated sigh. It aggravated him that he recognized Flynn's scent and touch, because the guy stole every possible opportunity to manhandle him. "Careful. Step up. The guy who likes to be stepped on is on the floor."

Kato flashed a smile he didn't feel toward Flynn's voice and easily walked across the guy on the floor to the sounds of guttural moans. At least he'd made one person's night. "Thanks for that. He should really warn people."

A soft laugh washed over Kato. He had to admit Flynn had a sexy accent. Scottish had always been his favorite. "I think he's hoping you'll trip over him and end up on the floor with him. If you ever do, you'll be quite literally fucked."

"Doubtful," Kato said, seeing his chance to shake Flynn's interest. "I bottom for no one."

"You'd be surprised how many men have said that to me. It never turns out to be true." Flynn's hard body pressed against his back. The man's lips touched the shell of Kato's ear. "I could make you beg."

He wanted to beg now—to be left in peace.

"Hey, Flynn. You've got a client waiting in room ten."

Kato had never been more grateful for Detroit's interference.

Flynn smoothed his hand down Kato's hip. "We'll finish this conversation later."

Kato bit back a growl and slipped inside his office. A sigh escaped him as the door clicked in place, putting a barrier between handsy Flynn and him. The moment he was alone, Kato dug out his phone and felt for the single button.

"Read unread messages."

"Brad: I forgot tomorrow was a work day. Since I don't get off until five, is it okay if I pick you up at seven?"

A smile touched Kato's lips. He pressed the button. "Text Brad. Seven is fine. My address is 3033 Lexington Way. What are you wearing right now?" As soon as Kato released the button, he burst into laughter. He hoped Brad read his text and smiled. After finding his chair, Kato sat and waited. Brad didn't make him wait long.

"Incoming text from Brad."

Kato couldn't push the button fast enough. "Read text."

"Brad: I just walked in the door, so I'm in the same clothes. Minus my jacket, of course. Give me five minutes and I'll be in the shower."

Kato closed his eyes and leaned back in his chair. He tried putting together an image of Brad in his mind based on Detroit's description. It seemed like it got harder and harder every day to picture things. He didn't want to forget what it was like to stare into someone's eyes. His wants didn't matter. It was all slipping away.

"Incoming text from Brad."

"Read text."

"Brad: What time do you get off tonight?"

With his eyes still shut, Kato brought the phone to his lips. "Text Brad. Whenever this place closes is when I'll get to leave. I'm somewhat trapped. Detroit is my ride home. Are you in that shower yet?" He released the button and immediately pushed it again. "Change settings to automatically read incoming texts for the next hour." There. As much as the high-tech phone gave him a slight sense of freedom, it could also be tedious and frustrating keeping up with every setting. In some ways, he was still learning to cope.

"Incoming text from Brad. Brad: If you're finished working and don't want to wait, I could take you home."

"Text Brad. You just got home. Take your shower. Think of me and tell me all about it later. I can't ask you to drive all the way back here."

Damn. Brad was already turning out to be amazing. Kato couldn't burden him the way he did Detroit. He wasn't helpless. If he got too tired, he could call a cab.

"Incoming text from Brad. Brad: I'll meet you halfway on this. My clothes are off and I'm stepping into the shower. When I'm done, I'll tell you all about it, if you'll let me tell you every detail while driving you home."

Kato bit his bottom lip and shook his head. Fuck his life. He wanted to see Brad again and the guy had just left. Kato released a loud sigh. "Text Brad. You've got a deal. I'll be finished here in an hour." He hoped he wasn't making a mistake. Nothing good came of seeming too eager, but damn. Kato really wanted to hear about that shower. He hoped it was steamy.

Kato got to work, finishing his duties for the night. He tried not to rush or count minutes in his head, but it was hard. The way his heart sped when a light knock landed on his office door gave away his excitement. "Come in." Kato bit his lip when he realized how breathless he sounded. When he heard the door open, a smile pulled at his lips.

"Wow. A man would do a lot to be greeted by that welcoming smile."

Kato's smile turned brittle as he realized it was Flynn. "What can I help you with?"

"Things are dying down out there. Would you like to get a drink?"

"Thanks, but I'm about to head out soon." He hoped.

"Oh." The heavy disappointment in Flynn's tone

had an ounce of guilt worming into Kato's heart. It wasn't that he didn't like Flynn. He just didn't like Flynn the way Flynn wanted. "I could give you a ride home."

"That's what I'm for," Brad said, appearing on the scene in a case of amazing timing, or terrible timing if he was the jealous type. No doubt Kato would learn which soon enough.

"Oh." Flynn's tone changed, becoming businesslike. "Then I guess my services aren't needed."

"Thanks for the offer," Kato said, flashing him a bright smile.

"Sure." Flynn's voice changed directions, as if he faced away. "See you later."

"See you." Kato held his breath and waited. Whatever happened next would tell him everything he needed to know about Brad. Kato felt it in his gut. Before Brad had time to speak, an unsettling knowledge overcame him. This was the first time he'd cared in years. It was also the first time he'd noticed that he hadn't cared before now. Brad was special somehow. Damn. Kato wasn't sure he knew himself anymore.

IT TOOK Brad a moment to realize they'd been staring at each other without speaking for an uncomfortably long while. A chuckle escaped him. He shook his head at his ridiculousness. Some form of primal possessiveness had crashed over him at the sight of the giant Scot flirting with Kato. He wasn't usually that guy. Now that they were alone, he felt a bit stupid.

"Sorry about that. I guess I shouldn't have sent your friend away."

"He's not my friend. How was your shower?"

"Crazy short," Brad admitted. Heat rushed to his cheeks. "I was in a hurry to get back here."

Kato's smile made the confession worthwhile. "Is it bad that I don't know whether I'm thrilled or disappointed? Even though I couldn't wait for you to get here, I really wanted to hear a steamy retelling of the events. Like, was there lots of soap and touching?"

Instant longing slammed into Brad. Kato was very sexual and unabashed. The way the words soap and touching rolled from Kato's tongue painted an immediate image in Brad's mind. "I could make something up, if you'd like." It was odd how much Brad wanted to please Kato. He hadn't felt that way in a long time. In truth, he'd thought Easton had killed that side of him. The side that would submit to someone else's will.

"I'd rather have the real thing," Kato said, pulling Brad back into their conversation and away from the edge.

Brad's brain stuttered to a stop. "Okay." For a split second, Brad wondered if it was his voice he'd heard, agreeing to something explicit with a stranger.

Kato stood. His fingertips trailed along the edge of his desk as he circled it, moving in Brad's direction. Brad didn't budge. He was too transfixed by the way Kato seemed completely focused on him. "Close the door."

Brad did as told. He would do anything.

Kato held his hand out, reaching for Brad. Brad found himself linking his fingers through Kato's and tugging him closer. Kato shuffled forward until their bodies collided. Brad couldn't look away from his face. It was set, showing his determination. They were well matched in height. Still, Kato's wide frame made him feel small.

"It's still Valentine's Day."

"It is."

Kato's expression was hot enough to incinerate the building. "You're not at home alone."

"There's that," Brad agreed.

"You should probably kiss me. That way you'll know if you're still interested enough—"

Brad kissed him, cutting off Kato's speech. He chuckled against Brad's lips. A spark of happiness lit inside Brad. He'd been unhappy for so long, he almost didn't recognize the sensation. Then Kato opened for him and their tongues met. Everything fell away. There was skill and then there were mind blowing experiences. Kato definitely fell into the second category. The unashamed way Kato had expected to hear about Brad's shower existed in his kiss. Brad wanted more.

Kato leaned away but didn't open his eyes. He looked turned on and sexy as sin. Brad couldn't look away. Kato's eyes opened, and their beauty punched Brad in the chest. "You have to keep our date now. Otherwise I might have to fight you. I'm joking, obviously," Kato added, as if Brad might think he'd actually fight him.

"I wouldn't miss it for the world."

Kato reached past Brad without looking away and killed the lights. "Are you ready?"

For so much, but not to leave Kato's company. He opened the door. "After you," Brad said, stepping aside and waving Kato ahead of him.

Kato didn't move. "Is it okay if I hold your arm? I

know my way to Payne's truck. He always parks in the same spot. Since I don't know where you parked..."

Brad held out his arm. "Okay." Even to his ears he sounded slightly confused. It was an odd thing to say.

An adorable smile hovered on Kato's lips. "You really can't tell, can you?"

"Um, tell what?" He hated sounding like an idiot, but Kato wasn't making sense.

Kato's smile grew. "I'm blind."

Brad's jaw dropped. It was the first time in his life for that reaction. He'd always thought it was just an expression for surprise, but it literally happened to him.

A sexy sounding chuckle escaped Kato. "I really wish I could see your expression right now."

After snapping his teeth together, Brad blinked a few times, hoping to gather his thoughts. He cleared his throat. "You're right. I can't tell. You've been looking right at me. It just didn't occur to me. Wow. I feel dumb."

Kato's smile slipped away. "Don't say that. I don't like that. You're not dumb just because you couldn't tell."

Warmth spread through Brad's chest. He

couldn't recall a time when anyone had been so instantly outraged on his behalf. Brad took Kato's hand and led it to the crook of his arm. "You don't have to ask for permission to touch me. I'd be proud for everyone to think you're leaving with me."

The bright smile that immediately stretched Kato's lips had Brad taking a deep breath. He chuckled. "I am leaving with you."

"Now everyone knows it," Brad said as he headed toward the door. He loved the sound of Kato's laughter.

"I have a feeling you're a bit of a nut."

Brad stroked the fingers curled around his bicep. "Actually, I'm pretty boring. Accepting Detroit's invitation is the most outrageous thing I've done in ages." He paused for half a beat as they reached the passenger side door of his BMW. Brad opened the door for Kato. "Are you truly ready to go home?"

"What did you have in mind?"

Brad helped Kato into the car. "Maybe I could show you my place. We could have some drinks and talk."

"I like you a lot," Kato said, flashing him a wicked smile. "You said 'show' me your place."

Brad shrugged, forgetting Kato couldn't see him. "I'm guessing you still see things in your own way.

Like through touch, or whatever. Honestly, I didn't consider my words."

The way Kato stared up at him from his spot in the car had Brad fighting back the urge to kiss him again. "That's why I like you, because you didn't pick through your words."

With a shake of his head, Brad closed the door. Kato was climbing into his mind and setting up shop. It was odd. He wasn't the type to get attached quickly. That didn't stop him from trying for more the moment he slid behind the wheel. "So, what's the verdict? Am I taking you home or would you like to spend a couple of hours with me?"

"I have nothing but an empty apartment waiting on me. You are an infinitely better choice."

Without a single thought or plan, Brad reached over, cupped the back of Kato's neck, and hauled him in for a kiss. There was no stopping it from happening. Kato had an inner light that Brad needed to touch. Like the first time they'd kissed, passion exploded the instant their lips met. By the time Brad pulled away, they were panting. For a moment, Brad stared into the face of hope, and he realized why Kato sucker punched him so hard. Brad saw everything he felt reflected back at him. He wasn't the only one who needed someone nice to come along. With all the dating apps and disconnect in the world, it was so damn hard to find this. It was impossible not to be completely terrified of himself and how badly he wanted Kato to be genuine.

"You should tell me about yourself while I drive." Even to Brad's ears he sounded turned on. "I need the distraction," he added with a chuckle, hoping to take the hard edge from his tone.

"Okay." Kato's open willingness had Brad's shoulders relaxing. He started the car while Kato picked a place to begin. "Let's see. I was born and raised in Santa Clara. In high school, I played every sport but landed a full-ride football scholarship at Washington State." Brad hung on every word as he drove. "Although I studied biomedical science with the idea of becoming an immunologist, I really had my sights set on playing pro. Then, I took a helmet to helmet hit and got a bad concussion. The next day, I woke up blind. They said, my brain had swelled and pressed too hard on the optical nerves, damaging them. So, I had to come back home and go back to living with my parents. It was an adjustment, to be sure. I only recently moved into an apartment alone."

Brad couldn't wrap his mind around the idea of waking up one day blind. All his dreams gone. "Wow. That had to be terrifying."

Kato's hands lifted before falling back to his lap. Brad saw the motion out of the corner of his eye. "I went through a long period of denial and didn't handle the news as well as I'd like to claim I did. Some days I'm still resentful as hell, but what choice do I have? Nobody asked me if I wanted this. All I can do is deal with it. You should probably start talking now before I make you think I'm a bitter waste of time."

"I can't even imagine. In your shoes, I think I would be a bitter mess. Hell, I'm pretty caustic now, and I'm not dealing with all that." Brad snapped his teeth together before he told too much. He counted to five and started over. "You already know about my job. I'm forty and my parents retired to Boca Raton three years ago. Since I'm an only child, I don't have anyone on this coast. It's just me and my job." Hearing his life out loud to someone new made Brad realize how boring he'd become. He never did anything anymore—like he'd given up. The last thing he wanted was to drag Kato into the mire he'd been living in the past year. "What's your favorite thing to do?"

"Go to the beach," Kato said without hesitation. "But I don't get to do it much anymore. I haven't found a feasible way to go alone and I hate asking people to go places with me. Poor Detroit. I've truly become his millstone the past couple of years."

Brad changed lanes before making a U-turn. "To the beach then."

"Are you joking?"

He glanced over and found Kato beaming. Brad knew he'd made the right choice. "Not at all. I'll do things with you. Anytime you want to do something and don't feel comfortable asking anyone else, call me."

"Okay."

Brad could tell by Kato's tone that he was humoring Brad. "I'm serious," Brad said, trying to drive his point home. "I don't have anyone to do things with. You need to help me out. I'm pitiful. All I do is sit at home and lament the fact I have no one to go anywhere with me, so I never go anywhere. You can't let me go on like this." He really liked Kato's laughter. Brad wanted more. "You know what else I haven't had in forever? Street fair food," Brad said without giving Kato time to guess. "You know how they always have that huge line of vendors down by—"

"Friar beach," Kato said at the same time as Brad said, "Friar beach. Exactly. I sure as hell don't want to do things like that alone."

"I miss that too."

An invisible weight—one Brad hadn't realized he'd been carrying—lifted from Brad's shoulders. He felt lighter and younger than he had in years. Kato touched his shoulder and followed the line of Brad's arm until he could link fingers with Brad. Brad glanced over in time to see Kato lean his way and settle in as if he felt every bit as comfortable in Brad's presence as Brad did in his. He couldn't recall the last time someone held his hand, especially when that person had reached for him first. It was such a small thing. He didn't want the night to end.

FRIAR BEACH WAS PACKED and noisy. Kato should've realized it would be since it was Valentine's Day. The smell of different high-calorie foods wafting through the air, combining with one another, brought on a wave of nostalgia. He'd come here all the time as a teen. In fact, he'd been asked to leave by the police a few times. His friends had been overprivileged hoodlums. Truth was he had been too. Those days and the person he'd once been felt like a lifetime ago.

Being there with Brad was a different type of

awesome. Brad was funny. He never moved away from Kato's side. It was the first time he'd met anyone who seemed to instinctively always know what Kato needed. He didn't push his help, but he also made sure Kato never panicked, which happened more than Kato liked to admit. In huge crowds and in places he was unfamiliar with—like where they were —Kato had a harder time keeping track of all the tricks he'd learned to keep his bearings. With Brad, he hadn't thought about it at all.

"Try this."

Kato leaned away. "What is it?"

"Nope," Brad said, laughing. "You have to trust me and try it. Open up."

With a shrug, Kato opened his mouth. Something warm, gooey, and sweet filled his mouth. He chewed while swiping at his lips. Kato swallowed. "Yum. Deep fried cookies. I can feel my arteries hardening."

"You're young. I think you can handle one." The laughter in Brad's voice kept Kato smiling until his cheeks ached. "Would you like to move closer to the water where it's less crowded?"

"Please?" Kato couldn't hide the desperation in his voice. He was a mess of nerves with everyone pressing in on them.

Brad took Kato's hand and steered him toward the sound of waves. "Step." Kato followed Brad's every command. "We're hitting the sand now." The sound of crashing water got closer until it drowned out everything else. Brad veered to the left, steering them along the water's edge. "This has been the best night I've had in a long time."

Kato nodded. "Me too. Do I hear music?" There was the merest hint of melody on the wind, but the farther they walked, the clearer the notes became. It was an old country love song. Kato didn't listen to country music, but it was a classic.

"There's a nightclub behind a hotel nearby." Brad stopped walking, bringing Kato up short. "May I have this dance?"

A snort escaped Kato. "Are you serious?"

"Of course," Brad said, as if dancing on the beach was a normal day for him. "No one is paying attention to us. I don't know if you realize this, but you have to be pretty shameless to be a lawyer."

"Really?" Even Kato heard the disbelief in his words.

"Yep. It's in the handbook," Brad said. He didn't wait for Kato to deny him. Brad's arms wound around Kato's neck. Kato's hands automatically landed on Brad's hips. Kato drew Brad closer. His heart sped. He loved the way Brad touched him constantly. No reservations. Back when he'd played ball, there'd been no shortage of willing bodies. People threw themselves at him all the time. He'd tried not to take advantage of anyone, but he loved sex as much as the next person.

This was different. Brad was different. Kato had changed a lot too. Physically and mentally. Overnight, people went from willing to respectful. He became part of a group he hadn't known existed. No longer was he seen as sexual unless it was someone's fetish. Equally, he'd stopped knowing what to look for in others, until now. Brad was checking all the boxes Kato hadn't known how to verbalize, even to himself.

His nerve endings lit up like a Christmas tree as Brad swept him into a slow dance. He didn't know if they matched any real rhythm. Kato was too busy feeling everything. Brad's breath against his ear. The light kisses he kept placing against its shell. The quiver in his stomach. He was acutely aware of the distance between his lips and Brad's skin. Kato could list the measurement of space between their bodies to the centimeter like a ruler. He craved. Hunger like he hadn't experienced in forever rose like a tidal wave. It was a thirst for life.

He hadn't felt truly connected to anyone in a while. Life had been muted since he'd lost everything. He'd gone numb. Kato wasn't sure he liked feeling again. There was too much hidden behind his wall.

"I should probably go home soon."

Kato swore he felt the happiness drain from Brad. He went still. "Okay. Sorry. I didn't think about the time."

Brad's unhappiness was heavier than Kato's fear. He couldn't take it. Before Brad could get away, Kato hauled him forward. Their bodies molded. His lips found Brad's. The terror that had slammed into him slipped away just as quickly beneath the sweetest kiss he'd ever experienced. He found himself clinging to Brad. The way their lips brushed tightened his chest. Brad held Kato's bottom lip between his teeth. They shared the same air. Something wet hit his face before another hit his arm. That's all the warning they got before the sky opened up, drenching them. Brad leaned away laughing. People screeched in the distance as they scrambled to get out of the rain. Kato didn't move. Even the cold rain couldn't deter him. Kato's arms tightened on Brad's waist.

Brad's laughter died. He stroked Kato's jaw. "I

thought you wanted to go home." Brad's tone was heavy with desire. Kato wanted to taste it.

"Later. I wasn't finished." Kato captured Brad's lips. This time, there was nothing sweet about their kiss. It was carnal. He wondered if steam rose from their bodies as the cold rain hit. Brad held his face as they fought to get closer. Kato felt every place they touched. He bit Brad's bottom lip and then sucked it in apology. A soft moan vibrated from Brad. Kato felt it to his soul. His lips moved to the corner of Brad's mouth and then to his cheek. Kato fought to catch his breath and calm his racing heart. Soon, he'd be alone in his apartment where he couldn't hide from his mind. Right now, in this moment and Brad's arms, he felt untouchable. Kato wished he could hang onto this forever. Maybe he could. Brad made him feel like anything was possible. Like he was still invincible. Or he could be again. Brad was a port in the storm Kato hadn't known he needed. Kato saw it now. He couldn't see anything else.

TWO

An image of Kato floated through Brad's mind. He touched his lips. Damn. It really had been one of the best nights of his life even if he had left Kato unmolested at his door. Those eyes. Goddamn. Kato's body. Fuck. He was in so much trouble. Brad couldn't recall liking someone so much so quickly. A shot of panic hit him, stealing his breath. He hoped Kato didn't cancel their date. There had been a moment on the beach when Kato seemed to lose interest or freak. Brad hadn't decided which. Either way, the moment passed as quickly as it hit. Then Kato kissed him. Damn. Brad caught himself before touching his lips again.

"Sorry," Cortland said as he finally answered the door Brad had been waiting at for ten minutes. "Sam and Bear were trying to break down the front door when the doorbell rang. I had to put them in the backyard, so they wouldn't run out. Please, come in." Cortland stepped aside, waving Brad inside the sprawling mansion. The home that belonged to the eccentric billionaire, Wyld West, was—to say the least—massive. It had probably taken Wyld's personal assistant ten minutes to walk from the front to the back to let the dogs outside.

"It's fine. In truth, I'm just happy to be out of the office. It's too nice of a day to be stuck inside."

Cortland nodded as he led the way through the house. "That's true. After this, Driver and I have plans to skip out the rest of the day and hit the pool."

"That sounds nice. How is your husband?"

Cortland flashed a smile over his shoulder. Happiness looked good on him. Before Driver came along, Brad didn't recall seeing Cortland smile. "He's good. Staying busy. What about you? How have you been?"

"Good," Brad automatically replied. He fought the urge to talk about Kato. This was a business call, and they weren't really friends. Brad swallowed his excitement. "I have two contracts to go over. One from John for you for the sketch he commissioned for Jonah." On top of being Wyld's personal assistant,

Cortland was also a famous artist John loved. Brad had to stop the man from spending his fortune on Cortland's work. "The other contract is for Wyld from Jude. It's some standard stuff about their partnership, sponsoring Hendrix for the special Olympics."

As they reached the kitchen, Cortland motioned for him to sit. "That's awesome. I'd forgotten about that one. How is Hendrix's training going?"

"Good," Brad answered honestly. Working for Jude and John Green offered him some interesting contract challenges with Jude married to an athlete and John being John. In one thought, Brad realized how boring he must be to others. No wonder Kato had a moment he'd obviously thought to run. Brad shook his head and got back on track. "He easily scored high enough in competition to represent the US."

"That's amazing." Cortland pulled out a chair across from Brad and sat.

Brad opened his briefcase and passed Cortland his contract. "Here's yours."

With a nod, Cortland opened the folder. His amber gaze skimmed the page and Brad scanned the room, trying not to stare. No one liked having someone watching as they read. Wyld had a gorgeous home. For such a huge and expensive place, it was lived in. There were signs everywhere that it housed a family. Shoes by the door. Papers on the fridge held by magnets. Drawings of hearts on a dry erase board. A smile tugged at Brad's lips. He was lucky to do business with so many good people. A lot of attorneys did crappy soul-sucking work with shady people. Brad was surrounded by people who loved each other.

A small movement at the edge of his vision had Brad turning his head. Through an open doorway, he spotted Wyld and Micah on the floor. It looked like they were having an indoor picnic. On a blanket, with his back against the wall, Micah sat reading. Wyld's head was in Micah's lap. Micah stared at an open book while running his fingers through Wyld's dark curls.

"Wyld's having a brainstorming session."

Brad tore his gaze away. Heat rushed to his face over getting caught staring. Cortland wasn't looking at him. He too stared in the couple's direction. Brad went back to watching them because he couldn't stop. "I think this is the first time I've ever seen Wyld sit still." It was true. Wyld fit his name. He was always on the move, getting into something.

36

"He says he thinks better on the floor. Personally, I think he's just eating up Micah's attention."

A smile pulled at Brad's lips. "What's he brainstorming?"

"Ideas for Micah's birthday. It's coming up, and he wants the day to be perfect."

Brad glanced Cortland's way. "Why doesn't he just ask Micah what he wants?"

Cortland focused on Brad. His amber gaze held its usual serious glint. "Micah's getting what he wants right now."

Brad's chest tightened with jealousy. He was blindsided by the emotion. Sometimes, at the most unexpected moments, he saw everything his life lacked. He dropped his gaze to his briefcase, hoping Cortland didn't see his feelings in his eyes. Brad wanted someone to love him that much where they desired nothing above spending time with him. It seemed like he was surrounded by people who had that. He had nothing. Not anymore.

No sooner than the dark thoughts hit, an image of Kato sneaked in again. The memory of the way Kato had kissed him, uncaring of the rain soaking them, reminded Brad he had hope. Perhaps there was someone out there for him. Maybe he'd already met him. A surprised sounding squeal rent the air.

Brad's chin shot up. Wyld had tackled a laughing Micah to the floor. Micah halfheartedly tried to get away while Wyld kissed him every place he could reach.

Cortland shot to his feet and closed the door. If Brad wasn't mistaken, Cortland blushed. "Let's just close this before we get a show. Wyld doesn't much care if people watch."

Brad couldn't stop smiling. Yeah. He was pretty sure he'd already met someone like that and they had a date tonight. Brad couldn't wait.

FOR THE FOURTH time in a few short minutes, Kato swiped his palms on his thighs. He wasn't nervous. At least, that's what he kept telling himself. When the knock finally came on his apartment door, Kato took a breath. He opened the door and the overwhelming scent of dark chocolate—like cocoa beans overcame him. He inhaled.

"Holy shit. What is that?"

A sexy chuckle caressed his ears. Kato's stomach cramped with hunger and not for sweets. "Believe it or not, it's flowers. Chocolate cosmos."

The way Kato's cheeks ached warned at how big

his smile had become. "Seriously? You brought me flowers?" He stepped aside, making room for Brad to pass.

"They're honestly not that pretty, but I asked the lady what the best and strongest smelling flowers were, and these were what she suggested. I think she made a great choice. The whole inside of my car smells like chocolate now. I'm thinking we should order dessert tonight."

The happiness in Brad's voice had Kato moving closer to the smell. He dragged the scent into his lungs as he reached out to touch them. He found a flower and rubbed the petal between his fingers. It was soft. "What color are they? I've never seen a chocolate cosmos."

"They're a dark red. Closer to burgundy. Damn near brown."

He dropped his hand. "Thank you. That's really nice. If you want, you can set them on the counter."

Considering how small his apartment was, he knew Brad wouldn't have any trouble finding the counter. The scent moved away. Kato fought the urge to follow them. He'd never met anyone like Brad. Flowers had never been his thing. Then again, no one had ever bought him flowers. It was nice—like Brad had thought about him. There was effort put into a gift that would die. Kato was feeling some shit in his chest about it. He found himself wanting to know all about Brad's day and whatnot.

"How was work?"

"It was good." Brad's voice moved closer again. "I spent most of my day at Wyld West's house, waiting for him to sign some paperwork."

"Sounds interesting." Honestly, Kato was only half listening while waiting for Brad to stop talking. He invaded Brad's space. His hands found Brad's waist. "I spent my day waiting too."

"Did you?" Brad's voice turned sultry.

Kato nodded as he slowly towed Brad even closer. "I checked the time a million times today."

"What had you so impatient?"

The laughter in Brad's voice had Kato's smile growing. "I shouldn't tell you, but there's this extremely sexy guy who asked me to dinner tonight."

"Oh dear. We have a problem then since you've already agreed to go with me."

"I guess you'll have to convince me you're the better choice," Kato said in mock boredom.

Brad's lips were so close, Kato could feel each breath he took. His hold tightened. Brad's voice lowered to nearly a whisper. "Let me see what I can do." Their lips met. Kato's heart sped. Even as their kiss turned heated, Brad's touch stayed respectful. Kato had no such qualms. His hands found Brad's ass. A moan rose in his throat at the perfection of the firm globes. He hauled Brad forward as he hardened, ensuring Brad felt how much he was desired. A voice in the back of his mind said he should slow down. Kato tried. His body refused to obey. He missed this. Being with Brad did wonders for his ego. He made Kato feel powerful. Kato's teeth sank into Brad's bottom lip. Brad gasped. The sound nearly crippled Kato. He was so goddamn horny he nearly demanded Brad drop to his knees. Instead, he pulled away and headed for the door.

"Okay. I'm convinced. You should take me dinner." In Kato's head, the words sounded cocky. Leaving his mouth, they were breathless.

As he reached the door, Brad overcame him. His body collided with Kato's back, molding against him. Brad's erection against Kato's ass had him swallowing a moan. The teeth scraping his neck had Kato clinging to the door for support. Brad sucked his skin, weakening Kato's knees. He cupped Kato's hard cock and shaped it through Kato's jeans, massaging. His touch immediately disappeared. "Okay. I'm ready."

Goddamn. Brad was perfect, and fuck. He gave

Kato exactly what he needed. Everything he missed...being made to feel like a man. Desired. It would be a long damn night, waiting to get his hands on Brad to show him who was really in charge.

IT WAS the longest dinner of Brad's life. He never quite lost the edge of lust Kato left him with after their kiss. It didn't help that Kato took every opportunity to touch him beneath the table, making it hard for him to concentrate on the stories they shared. By the time he had Kato backed against his front door, kissing him, Brad was ready to burst from his skin. He was hooked, and Kato knew it. The surety in which Kato touched him proved the man already understood his power over Brad. But Brad had years of patience and experience on his side. He intended to use it.

"You should come in," Kato whispered between kisses.

Brad pulled away just enough to touch his forehead to Kato's. He adored the man's blue eyes. They were beautiful. "There's nothing I would love more than to come in, but I want you to call me again."

A smile exploded across Kato's face. "You don't think I'll call you again if you come in."

"Nope," Brad said, not pulling any punches. He honestly believed if he slept with Kato tonight, it would the last time they'd see each other. Even though Kato touched him with confidence, occasionally he looked ready to bolt. Right now, lust kept him hanging around. "I think you'll use me and throw me away."

Kato straightened away from the door. "Then I guess it's a good thing I don't need anyone to keep me satisfied."

Brad nearly groaned aloud. He almost caved, but he liked Kato too much. "One more kiss and I'll leave you to it."

Kato made his one kiss count. Brad was left breathless and limping. By the time he made it back to his car, Brad wondered if anyone would judge him if he cried. He also hoped he hadn't made a huge mistake. There was a real possibility he might not hear from Kato again, sex or not. He might've missed his chance. His phone rang at the end of the street. Seeing Kato's name, Brad swallowed a laugh and answered.

"Hello?"

"So, I went to dinner with that super sexy guy. He doesn't think I'll call again."

Brad switched the call to hands-free. He couldn't stop smiling. "Seriously? What an ass. As it happens, I also had a date with a really hot guy. I asked him to spend the day with me on Saturday."

"What did he say?" Brad could hear the smile in Kato's voice.

"I don't know. What do you say?" Brad held his breath, hoping.

"Do you plan to leave me at the door miserable again?"

Brad took a breath. He didn't know if he could wait until Saturday. "No. I intend to have you in every way you'll let me."

"Then it's a date. Are you home yet?"

"Almost," Brad said as he turned onto his street.

Kato made a humming noise that had Brad's already hard dick leaking. "Let me know when you're parked. I'm toying with my flowers, feeling of their shape and getting a mental picture of them. I don't think they're ugly."

Damn. He wanted to turn the car around. "They're not. They're unusual. Just like you. I'm pulling into the garage."

"You think I'm unusual?"

Brad put the car in park and killed the engine. He turned the key toward him so Kato's voice could fill the speakers still. He loved the sound of Kato's voice surrounding him. "For me, you are." He leaned his head back and closed his eyes. An image of Kato filled his mind. "We live in a world of online dating and one-night stands. People don't need anyone anymore. The moment they're dissatisfied, someone else is a swipe away. I don't suit that life. I don't think you do either."

"No, but maybe not for the reasons you think. Are you out of sight?"

A smile tugged at Brad's lips. "Yes."

Kato made the sexy humming noise again that Brad loved so much. "Good. I don't like to share. I'm stripping." The sound of something brushing the phone let Brad know Kato wasn't only teasing him. The clothes were coming off. "Have you ever jacked off in your car?"

A surprised laugh escaped Brad. "No. Not that I recall."

"You do strike me as the proper type... most of the time. I think you'd do a lot with the right kind of motivation though." Kato's breathless tone made Brad wonder if he was touching himself. He wanted to ask. Bravery fled.

"What sort of motivation?"

"I think you like to be told what to do."

Brad bit his bottom lip. He was so fucking turned on he was ready to explode. Kato was more right than Brad wanted to admit. Brad was an outgoing person. An independent person. But when it came to sex, that's when he lost the nerve to be as free as he wished. He'd always believed that was why he'd lost Easton. That's why Easton had gotten bored.

"Maybe I'm just not that exciting," Brad admitted out loud as if Kato heard his thoughts about Easton.

"Maybe you've let other people convince you of that because they're lacking. I fall short in a lot of ways, but not in this."

"I don't think you fall short in anything. In fact, you're as close to perfect as I've seen in a long time." Brad was being honest. In fact, Kato was so flawless he scared Brad a little.

Kato didn't call him a liar, but he didn't acknowledge Brad's claim. "I doubt, if I asked, you'd give me a list of what you enjoy sexually."

"You'd be right," Brad admitted with a chuckle that sounded nervous even to him. He was showing the side of himself he hated. The side that bored people.

"It's okay, sexy. I know what you need. Like I said, I excel in this area. Let me guess, you love being on your knees."

Brad's stomach twisted with want. He swore he could already taste Kato. "Yes."

"Unzip your pants."

Brad did as commanded. His underwear was soaked with pre-cum. He needed this—to be told what to do and how to let go. "Okay."

"Don't stop there, Brad. I want your pants and underwear around your knees with no fucks given to those precious leather seats."

While taking measured breaths, Brad pushed his pants and underwear down. Embarrassment tried creeping in despite being shut away inside his garage where no one could see. "Anything you want."

"That's what I like to hear. What I don't like hearing is that hint of shame in your voice. Stop. You're not allowed to be embarrassed with me. I'll never judge you or let anyone else find fault in anything you do, especially when you're doing it for me. Understood?"

Brad nodded, forgetting for a moment Kato couldn't see him. Kato wove a spell with his voice, stealing pieces of Brad. "I understand."

"Good." A hiss escaped Kato, making Brad's

stomach muscles clench. "My dick is in my hand and you're in my head. I expect the same."

Brad palmed his cock, half expecting to blow the second he fisted himself. "You're incredibly sexy."

"I know you have me on speaker," Kato said, ignoring his compliment. "Both those hands are free. Use them. Toy with those balls and finger that asshole while you stroke your cock. I want to hear your pleasure."

He slid down in the seat, spreading his knees wider. A moan escaped him as he pumped and squeezed.

"Good boy," Kato praised. His voice turned guttural. "Run your thumb across your slit. Feel your pre-cum. That's for me and what I can do for you." Brad followed every order. "Do you like to be seduced and slowly fucked? Or would you prefer I bend you over the first piece of furniture I find and fuck you hard?"

"I want both," Brad admitted, because once with Kato would never be enough. He needed everything.

"I can do that." Pressure climbed Brad's shaft at the promise in Kato's voice. "I like to bite, Brad. You'll have to accept that."

Another moan tore from Brad's throat at the confession. He could practically feel Kato's teeth sinking into him. Brad was too close to the edge to watch his tongue and Kato had told him not to be embarrassed. "I like having my ass smacked."

A low moan sounded through the speakers. "Thank fuck, because I can't wait to do that. You've got me so hot, sexy. I won't last much longer. Come for me. Shoot your load with my name on your lips. I need it."

Brad's hips lifted. He pumped faster as he moved against his hand. Whimpers left him as he struggled toward the edge. His muscles tensed. He tugged on his dick, needing relief from the madness. A cry tore from his throat as the first wave hit. Jet after jet of cum shot from him, bringing release. Kato's name left his lips and would have even if Kato hadn't demanded it. Brad had never wanted anyone more. He didn't doubt it now. No one else had ever tempted him into such a hot encounter. A cry sounded through the phone, sending another wave crashing over him as Kato cried his name. Brad fought for air, trying to come down from his high. He couldn't think straight.

"Damn," Kato cursed. "I wish I could kiss you. Not getting to taste my name on your lips is torture. You taste so good."

Brad squeezed his eyes shut and clung to the

moment. Saturday. He'd see Kato on Saturday. It felt so far away. He felt too much. "I miss you." Goddamn. It was ridiculous. He shouldn't need someone so much after such a short period of time, but Kato was amazing.

"I think I might be in trouble, Brad."

Brad's eyes flew open at the fear in Kato's voice. He didn't think Kato was the type to show his heart. He stared at his dashboard and held his breath. Brad needed Kato's words like he needed oxygen to survive.

"I like you more than I should."

Brad sucked in a breath at the confession, making himself lightheaded. He didn't hesitate to give the words back. "Me too. I wasn't expecting you."

"Same."

Dropping his head back against the seat, Brad stared at the ceiling of his car. He didn't know where they were headed. All Brad knew was, he didn't want things to end. He hadn't been this hopeful in a long time. He hadn't been this terrified either.

THREE

Kato: *Do you mind picking me up from work instead of my place? Detroit scheduled five tours this morning, so I had to come in for a bit. Plus, I really couldn't turn down the extra money.*

Brad: *No problem. I need to swing by my office to drop off some paperwork. Can't wait to see you. I'll be there soon.*

Kato: *I can't wait to see you either.*

Brad couldn't stop smiling like a goddamn idiot. Wyld had finally gotten around to signing his contracts. All Brad had to do was drop them off at work so his team could get started putting things in motion, and he'd be with Kato. As he pushed his way through the door at Green's Fighter Fuel, he ran headlong into Jake. His smile slipped away. Jake was

Easton's brother. Working in the same building was uncomfortable as hell for both of them. For the first few months after the breakup, Jake had seemed determined to make Brad's life hell. It hadn't taken long for him to get bored when Brad hadn't reacted to his goading. Not to mention, fucking with Brad was skating thin ice, since—technically—Brad was his boss.

"Hey," Brad said, trying to sound polite and detached.

Jake's dark green gaze so much like Easton's skirted down Brad's body with open disdain. "Hey. I wasn't expecting to see you today."

Brad headed for his office. "Just dropping off some paperwork," he said over his shoulder. To his irritation, Jake followed. "You might want to hurry. Easton will be here any second. We're going to lunch."

"That's nice." Brad made himself proud with how unconcerned he sounded. The last thing he wanted was to run into Easton when he was having such a great morning. He'd be with Kato soon, Brad reminded himself. Brad dumped his files on his desk. He'd call his assistant later and let him know he'd dropped off the contracts. No need to hang around any longer than necessary. He locked his door behind him. Only his assistant Shaun and the owners had access to his office. As one of the company's legal aides, it irritated Jake to no end that Shaun had more access to Brad's files than he did. That's exactly why Brad always limited his reach.

He barely spared Jake a glance. "Have a good weekend." Brad didn't look back on his way out. He almost made it. His car was within sight.

"Brad?"

His shoulders fell. It was out of his control. The sound of his name on Easton's lips was like getting hit by a two by four. No amount of inner pep talks could help him as he glanced over and set eyes on the man who'd once meant everything to him.

Easton wore a soft looking V-neck gray t-shirt and low-slung jeans. His green eyes always looked sad, woeful. He made people want to comfort him and fall in love. The fucking rat bastard. Today, Brad felt nothing. An invisible weight lifted from his shoulders. "Easton," he said, hearing his disinterest for the real emotion it was. With a nod, he kept moving.

Easton didn't let up. He followed on Brad's heels. "How have you been?"

Brad reached for his door handle determined for Easton to know he was in a hurry. "Good. How's

Rob?" He couldn't resist. Some bitterness ran too deep.

Easton winced. "That's been over for a long time."

No doubt it had been over for the same length of time as Easton had been without Brad's financial support. Easton came from a good, wealthy family, but he didn't like to work as much he enjoyed spending. Still, Brad didn't know how to respond. There was nothing left to say, so he stared at Easton and let the silence grow until Easton shifted uncomfortably from one foot to the other. He truly was gorgeous. Brad recognized Easton's beauty in the same way he noticed an expensive car he didn't care to buy.

"Well, it's been good seeing you," Easton said, sounding like he meant the claim. He nodded toward the building. "I guess I'd better meet Jake. He's waiting."

Brad gave him a sharp nod. "Yes. He is."

Easton backed away, chewing his bottom lip. Brad tore his gaze away from the practiced move. He had someone real waiting for him. Someone who didn't practice fake expressions in the mirror. Brad climbed in his car without a backward glance. He doubly needed to see Kato.

Despite his better judgment, Brad found his gaze sliding Easton's way as he pulled from the lot. Easton hadn't budged. He stood, staring Brad's way and looking lost. Brad shook his head. He didn't understand Easton at all.

As Brad passed through the door of the Den of Payne, Easton was already forgotten. Brad could almost feel Kato already. They were under the same roof. He was seconds away from getting to touch him.

"Hey, Brad. It's good to see you."

Brad drew up short as Detroit called his name and jogged across the empty playroom where he'd first met Kato. Detroit's welcoming smile had Brad returning the gesture. "Hey." He held his hand out to shake Detroit's.

Detroit heartily accepted, damn near shaking the teeth from Brad's head in his enthusiasm. "What brings you by? Have you decided to accept my invitation and become a full member?"

"Um," Brad said, dragging out the word. He wasn't sure how to respond. It was possible he wouldn't be welcomed inside the exclusive club to keep picking up Kato without securing a membership before long. "Actually, I'm here to pick up Kato."

"That was my second guess," Detroit said, openly laughing. He was such a friendly person. Detroit sucked people in, making them want to know him better. "He's in his office. It's none of my business, but since I get partial credit for you two meeting in the first place, I'm giving my opinion. You two look great together."

Brad's smile grew. It was out of his control. "Thank you."

Detroit turned serious. It happened fast—like Brad stared at someone new. "Take it easy on his heart, okay? Life has had a real field day kicking him the last couple of years."

Brad matched Detroit's countenance. This was Kato's friend. He deserved reassurance. "It's had a grand time fucking me too. I like Kato a lot."

Detroit's smile returned. "That's good. I know he's grown and doesn't need my protection, but I can't help it, you know?"

"Yeah. I get it. So," Brad said, glancing toward Kato's office. "He's in his office, you say?"

"Yep. You two have fun doing whatever and let me know about that membership. It might be fun." Detroit winked as he slapped Brad across the back and walked away.

Brad watched him go. He had no clue why

Detroit thought he would enjoy this place, but Brad was damn glad he'd accepted the invitation. Otherwise, he wouldn't have met Kato. Giving up trying to figure out Detroit's thought process, he headed for Kato's office. The door stood open. He spotted the giant Scot from the other day first. He leaned over Kato's shoulder, staring at something on Kato's desk. As Brad looked on, Flynn spoke against the shell of Kato's ear. Kato leaned away, visibly trying to put distance between them. Even so, jealousy clawed at Brad's gut. He wanted to be the only person in Kato's space.

"Here we are again," Brad said, making his presence known. "You hang out in here a lot."

Flynn didn't get in a hurry to back away from Kato. In fact, his eyes screamed he was up for a challenge as he slowly straightened away from Kato's desk. "I see you've come to steal Kato from underneath me again." He enunciated just the right places to ensure Brad caught his drift. Not only did he want Kato, the guy thought he could easily take Kato from Brad.

Kato's smile made Brad forget his irritation. "Hey. I can't tell you how ready I am to get out of here."

Flynn winked as he went by, confusing Brad. As

Brad's gaze swung back Kato's way, he let it go. "Your chariot awaits."

Kato pushed to his feet. He trailed his fingertips along the desk as he circled it, moving in Brad's direction. Brad measured each breath as Kato crossed the room. He didn't hesitate to take the man's hand the instant Kato reached for him. Brad towed him closer until their bodies met. "Goddamn. I missed you," Brad breathed as their lips met. The universe seemed to click. Everything fell into place— like he'd been waiting on Kato his entire life.

Kato hummed. The sound vibrated on Brad's tongue, making his heart beat faster. "I didn't think today would ever get here." Kato's confession had Brad's happiness level shooting through the roof. He found himself rushing Kato to the car. It was a move he wouldn't have noticed if Kato hadn't squeezed his arm as if fighting to hang on and keep up.

Brad slowed his step. "Sorry. I guess I'm in a bigger hurry to have you to myself than I realized."

The way Kato smiled, showing his open humor over Brad's impatience, helped ease the tension. It came back with a vengeance when Kato used Brad's opening the car door for him as an opportunity to openly stroke him through his jeans. Brad closed the door and braced his hands against the roof. He fought for control. Kato's evil grin didn't help matters. Brad spent a moment staring at him. Those blue eyes. That sexy jaw covered in stubble. Fuck. Brad could already feel the beard burn. He circled the car wondering why teleportation wasn't a thing yet.

"I thought you were in a hurry." The laughter in Kato's voice had Brad grinding his back teeth. Kato laughed harder. "I can feel your glare."

A snort escaped Brad as he pulled from the lot. He'd never been happier to be tied into knots by someone. They rode in silence with Brad hyperaware of the way Kato toyed with his fingers. The flutter in his chest was either the beginnings of an arrhythmia or feelings. Either way, he was in big trouble.

The door to the garage closed behind them. A hum sounded from Kato's throat. "The infamous garage. Damn." He opened his car door and Brad dropped his forehead to the steering wheel. It was like Kato was determined to cripple him. Brad had never met anyone so sexually powerful. He made Brad weak.

His door opened, and Kato's hand appeared palm up. "Let's go, sexy."

Brad's palm slid across Kato's. Kato's hand closed

around his. Brad's breath caught. There was no fear or reservation in Kato's expression. His confidence fed Brad.

He led Kato toward the back door. "There are three steps." With a nod, Kato navigated the steps. Once inside, he set Kato free. "Feel free to explore."

"Why is there no furniture in here?"

Brad glanced around in surprise. They'd only made it five steps inside. "How did you know that?"

Kato smirked, as if he enjoyed shocking Brad. "Your footsteps sound hollow—like you're walking through an empty room."

He took Kato's hands and walked backward. "I've only lived here a year."

"That doesn't explain why you don't have furniture."

"My ex got the furniture," Brad said as he sat on the couch. He tugged Kato close until he stood between Brad's knees. "I got to be free of a cheating dick."

"Ouch."

Brad ran his hands up the back of Kato's thighs until he cupped his ass. Damn. Kato's body was delicious. Since Kato wasn't stopping Brad from touching him, Brad didn't quit. He leaned forward and kissed Kato's stomach. "I'm not bitter. I have what furniture I need. Right now, with you, it's feeling a lot like I got the better end of the deal."

Kato buried his fingers in Brad's hair and held on. Brad's lips skimmed Kato's stomach again. He heard Kato release his breath. With one sound, Brad knew Kato was every bit as turned on and impatient as Brad. Kato led Brad's hands to the button of his jeans. "It's time. Don't you think?"

Brad popped Kato's button loose. He slid down his zipper. "Yes."

Showing zero hesitation, Kato pulled his shirt up and over his head before tossing it toward the couch. Brad licked his lips and concentrated on breathing. Kato's body was amazing. Even though Kato didn't play football any longer, he'd obviously not given up staying in shape. Brad wanted to touch him everywhere. He set Kato's erection free. Damn, even that part of his body was beautiful. Brad's mouth watered. Kato's chin hit his chest. Brad felt the power shift.

"Should I give you a tour?"

A chuckle that sounded evil even to Brad's ears escaped him when Kato growled. His fingers found Brad's hair. He slowly towed Brad forward, leading him to his dick. Brad licked him. His stomach muscles tightened as if he'd been the one to get his cock licked. Kato's thumb found Brad's jaw, as if he needed to feel the way it moved as Brad took Kato down his throat. The sound Kato made as Brad's throat tightened around him made goosebumps rise on Brad's skin. That one strangled moan mimicked everything Brad felt.

"Goddamn. You're perfect. Stand up."

After one final bold lick, Brad stood. He couldn't look away from the flush on Kato's cheeks. Kato's fingers found the hem of Brad's shirt. He dragged the material upward until he worked it over Brad's head. After tossing it aside, Kato skimmed his fingertips down Brad's torso. Brad fought the urge to suck in his stomach. He didn't look like Kato. For one thing, he was older. Kato had youth on his side. Brad had gravity on his.

Kato's expression turned even more heated as he reached the button of Brad's jeans. "I want you more than I can remember ever wanting anyone." Brad hung on every word while feeling every touch. Kato worked the button loose and slid Brad's zipper down. "Sometimes, I think you forget I have no real idea of what you look like, but you're still the sexiest man I've ever met." Brad's eyes burned, making him realized he hadn't blinked. Kato had every ounce of his attention. "It's just you," Kato said almost whispering. "Your kindness and your voice. That sexy laugh and your moments of awkwardness." Kato smiled. Brad lost a piece of himself. He felt it happen —like Kato had picked his pocket, except it was a far more valuable loss. Brad had a feeling he'd find out the hard way one day what this moment cost. "I don't want to be with anyone else." At Kato's final confession, Brad's breath left his lungs in one hard whoosh.

"Me either." Even to Brad's ears the words sounded like a vow.

"Good." Kato looked serious and hard. "Because you're mine." He palmed Brad's erection as he staked his claim. "I don't share." He pumped, weakening Brad's knees. "You say your ex was a cheat. That's something you don't have to fear with me, but you should know I'm jealous and possessive." Brad went cross-eyed as Kato shoved his jeans down and went two hands in, massaging Brad's balls as he pumped Brad's cock. "But you'll never have to worry about going unsatisfied. You should sit on my dick."

"Goddamn." The curse sounded like a benediction leaving Brad's lips. If Kato was half as hot in bed as he was standing around talking, then Brad was in deep. "There's lube and condoms in the bedroom. This way." He took Kato's hand and led him toward the bedroom. "I rearranged the living room to match yours, so you won't have to adjust. But where you have a wall to the left of your couch, you'll find my bedroom. If you walk straight, you'll hit the bed."

"You get sexier every time you open your mouth."

Brad bit his lip, fighting a smile at the praise. It seemed like everything he did and every reaction he had anymore were all for Kato. "The bed is only maybe twenty steps."

"So, we're there?"

"Yes." At Brad's answer, Kato shoved, pushing Brad facedown onto the bed. His lips found the small of Brad's back. Brad bit the comforter. Kato tore at Brad's clothes. He touched every place he bared. His fingertips skimmed Brad's ass crack before he toyed with Brad's asshole. "Oh, god." The cry escaped him without thought. Kato owned him.

"You promised there would be condoms and lube."

"Um," Brad said, trying to gather his bearings. He glanced around. "Reach to your right." Kato did as told. His fingertips landed on the bedside table. "There's a drawer right there. Everything is inside."

Kato opened the door and felt around inside.

There were more than those two items inside. Kato's face never turned away from Brad, giving Brad the freedom to enjoy his every reaction. Kato smirked. "We'll explore this drawer a lot further another day. For now," he said, coming out with a condom, "I need inside you." He finished stripping and ripped into the condom. Brad watched him suit up and dive back inside the drawer for the lube. He found everything easily and with a confidence that was sexy as sin. He coated his sheathed cock with lube. Brad's stomach muscles tightened. It had been a damn long time since he'd had sex.

Kato's hands slipped up the backs of Brad's thighs. "I think I let you cool down too much. You feel like you're ready to bolt."

"No." Brad meant it. Kato was fucking him today even if the house caught fire. "As you've pointed out, I'm awkward." To his horror, a nervous chuckle escaped along with the confession. He buried his face in the covers. A solid full handed slap landed on his ass cheek. Brad's cock soaked the covers beneath him with pre-cum. A moan ripped from his throat.

"You're not allowed to be ashamed. That's already been agreed upon."

Brad sucked air. "I know."

"On your knees." Brad tucked his knees beneath

him and Kato bit his ass. He sucked hard enough to leave a hickey on Brad's ass cheek. Brad scratched at the covers, fighting the urge to beg. Without warning, Kato's tongue found his asshole. He licked. Brad tugged at his cock. He couldn't stop it from happening. If Kato didn't give him relief soon Brad's mind would snap.

"Please?" The plea was out of his control.

Kato shifted onto his knees behind Brad and probed at Brad's hole with his dick. Brad moved against him, silently begging. Kato pushed inside. A moan tore from Brad's throat. Kato pushed deeper. Brad's cock leaked pre-cum onto the bed like a faucet.

"Fuck." Kato's curse had Brad stroking himself faster. "You're so hot and tight." Kato pumped inside him, changing angles to hit the perfect spot. Brad made sure Kato heard his pleasure even though it cost him air he couldn't spare. "I have a confession." Brad wondered how in the hell Kato talked so much while he could barely think. "It's been a long time since I've done this, so I'm not going to last. You need to come for me, sexy. I want to feel it happen."

Brad squeezed his eyes shut and committed every second to memory. He relished every sensation. Pressure built and climbed. He didn't slow. Kato had told him to come. It was Brad's job to make him happy now. He cried out as the first wave hit. Brad pumped faster, needing more.

"That's it. Holy shit, Brad. You feel fucking amazing. Goddamn. I can't hold out." A strangled cry escaped Kato. He pressed his forehead to Brad's back as he slammed inside him. His fingers dug into Brad's sides, holding him in place. Brad had never been prouder. Kato collapsed, taking Brad down with him. He didn't stay that way. Kato turned Brad in his arms and held him. His lips skimmed Brad's cheek before finding Brad's lips. Brad's eyes stung. He didn't think anyone had ever kissed him as sweetly after sex. Kato's kiss changed the dynamics of the entire encounter. He'd been fucked—hard, but that goddamn kiss twisted everything. They'd made love.

He nibbled Kato's bottom lip. Kato chuckled, making Brad's heart do a happy flip. "I need you to point me to a trash can."

"Let me give you the grand tour." Brad slipped from the bed and tugged Kato to his feet. He couldn't stop smiling. Kato was so sexy, and Brad had that. Damn. It was unreal. "This can be your side of the bed, if you like. That way you'll always have a starting point. Remember that bedside table," he said, not giving Kato a chance to say he wouldn't be back. Brad couldn't consider the possibility right now. He kept a light hold on Kato's hand, leading him while still giving him the freedom to find things himself. "Follow the table." He slid Kato's fingertips across the table. "At the edge is a doorway." Brad helped him find the frame. "This is the bathroom. Everything is super simple in here. It's a straight line. Vanity, trash can, toilet, and shower." He walked backward, hovering his hand over Kato's down the line. After he'd taken Kato all the way to the walk-in shower, he moved toward the door. "I'll grab a towel. They're behind the bathroom door, if you're looking for the linen closet. I'll leave you alone and clean up our mess. Do you want a bottle of water?"

Kato's hand shot out. He snagged the back of Brad's neck and hauled him forward. His mouth covered Brad's in a breathtaking kiss. When Kato pulled away, he looked more confident than any man should. He didn't release his hold on Brad's nape. "Stop. I swear I can hear your thoughts churning. I'm not going anywhere."

Brad took a breath. Until Kato called him on it, he hadn't realized how much his panic had risen. "I know."

"Good," Kato said before kissing him again. This

time it was a slow, hot kiss that left Brad breathless. Kato thumb brushed Brad's bottom lip. "I'd love a bottle of water."

Brad dipped his chin and Kato released him. Without a backward glance, Brad dug out a towel. He was scared if he looked at Kato, he'd go on the attack. Brad didn't know how to stop. He'd been so long without love in his life, he longed for more than he should. It was time to clean their mess, get some water, and get ahold of his heart. Kato probably wouldn't want him forever and that was okay. Now all he needed to do was tell himself that a thousand more times. Maybe then he'd believe he would survive the loss.

KATO RETRACED HIS STEPS, learning his way around. As his fingertips skirted the bedside table, he felt the slight cold radiating from a bottle of water. He fought a smile. Brad blew him away. The man had no clue how amazing and unique he was. He'd rearranged the furniture for fuck's sake. Who did that? Not only had Brad rearranged his entire house to suit Kato, he'd done so causally, as if it meant nothing.

Kato's smile fell. He wondered if Brad realized how telling his actions were. It was obvious Brad was used to living while bent over backward for others—like it was expected he would always have to do more than any one person should. Kato took a drink. If Brad was watching him, Kato didn't want the man to see his aggravation. Even he didn't understand how Brad's actions could make him ecstatic and furious at the same time.

"You should never wear clothes," Brad said from the bed, proving Kato had been right to suspect he was staring. "I could watch you all day."

Kato set his knee on the mattress and climbed into bed, scooting until he found himself wrapped in Brad's arms. He snuggled in, happy to be held. "I imagine it would be frowned upon by most if I never wore clothes. Not to mention, where I work, things happen."

Brad's chuckle sounded loud against Kato's ear with his cheek pressed to Brad's chest. His fingertips brushed up and down Kato's arm, relaxing him. "I have to be honest," Brad said, suddenly, as if fighting himself. "It bothers me a little, knowing you work at a sex club, especially because of that guy who's always hanging on you when I show up. It's stupid, I know."

"You know I can't see anything that goes on there, right?" Even Kato heard the humor in his tone. He had to keep things light. It wasn't that he didn't care about Brad's feelings. Kato had to work, and it wasn't easy finding a job when he couldn't see. His fingers found Brad's stomach. He slid his hand lower. Just enough to tease. They needed to move away from this topic. "Besides, all I think about is you while I'm there." Kato traced a line from Brad's navel to his hip bone and back again. "This morning, I heard moans traveling down the hall. I could tell they were faked. Yours are so real. I get that I'm lucky to have met you."

Brad's voice sounded deeper when he responded, proving Kato's touch was getting to him. "This sounds like bullshit you made up to change the subject, but that's okay. It means a lot that you're willing to talk shit to make me happy. Don't worry. I won't be handing you an ultimatum one day. I know it's just a job." Brad shifted beneath him. "In fact, if you could forget I said anything, that would be great."

Kato shouldn't have laughed. He couldn't stop it from happening. "You're so deliciously weird." Kato shifted to his knees before straddling Brad's hips. "And sexy," he added. With his hands braced against the bed, Kato leaned in and kissed Brad's throat. "Just overall delicious," Kato growled against Brad's skin.

Brad's hands landed on Kato's hips. His breathing deepened. "Damn. You blow me away."

Kato moved lower and nibbled on Brad's collarbone. "Oh, you're about to get blown." He felt more than heard Brad's breath catch. Kato soaked in the sensation. He couldn't let Brad dwell on being disappointed in Kato's job. Kato was unhappy enough with his life for the both of them. He needed his time with Brad to be an escape. Nothing else in his life held an ounce of peace. Brad was steady and strong. He quieted Kato's raging mind. Kato wanted more. He needed Brad.

FOUR

"Time to get up lazy bones."

A groan escaped Kato. He had a hard time with sleeping hours since losing his sight. Sometimes he slept opposite hours by mistake. "What time is it?"

"Six thirty."

Kato's head popped up. "In the morning?"

Brad bounced on the bed, shaking Kato around. "Yep. Let's go."

"What the fuck? Why? Are you even human?"

Brad straddled his ass, pinning him to the bed. His lips skimmed Kato's nape. "Come on, sexy. I promise I'll get you coffee on the way to the beach. You don't want to miss the sunrise."

Kato buried his head under the pillow and growled. "I can't see, so no thanks. I'd rather sleep."

"Nope," Brad said, stealing the pillow and tossing it aside. His lips found Kato's nape again. "I know you can't see with your eyes. But your skin still feels the light change, filling the shadows. Your ears still hear the slight shift in the waves." Brad sucked his earlobe. "Your tongue still tastes my kisses while the sand is between your toes."

Kato tried groaning again, but it sounded like a moan instead.

Brad kissed the spot below Kato's ear. "You said your favorite thing to do was go to the beach. My favorite thing to do is to make you smile. You can sleep on a blanket while soaking up the sun. I won't stop you, but you're getting a day at the beach."

"Fine." Even Kato heard the petulance in his voice as he tried getting up. He didn't mean it. Sometimes, he thought he shouldn't let Brad know how happy he was with him. Good things had a habit of slipping away from him. With another quick kiss, Brad set him free.

"Hurry," Brad called at his back.

"On it." Because, honestly, there was nothing he wouldn't do to keep the happiness in Brad's voice. Inside the bathroom, he stubbed his toe on the vanity four steps in when he miscalculated how far he'd walked. Kato bit the inside of his cheek and swallowed down a round of cursing. Fuck. He hated this bullshit. It was impossible to keep track of every place in his head. He'd be goddamned if he used one of those white canes everywhere he went. Kato rushed through his morning routine to the best of his ability. The whole time he pep talked himself, hoping to shake off the black mood trying to swallow him. Brad deserved more from him than the bitter mess he became when no one was watching. It was a trip to the beach. He couldn't recall the last time anyone had offered to take him some place to make him happy. Much less demanded it. By the time he left the bathroom, he was still completely nude, but his mood was better.

"Damn. Now, you're making me want to go back to bed."

Kato smiled at the hunger in Brad's voice. Brad was completely incapable of any sort of artifice. "I'm up now. My baby is getting his sunrise."

The happy laughter coming from the bed had Kato's smile turning real. "I put your bag on the bed." Kato moved to the bed's edge and felt for the bag. He rubbed each item between his thumb and forefinger, finding the clothes he wanted. Kato hated how long it took him to do everything, but he was getting better, and he could do it alone. That mattered a lot.

It helped that Brad chattered the entire time about some restaurant that served brunch that looked out over the ocean as if he didn't notice Kato's struggle.

"How are we doing on time?"

"I have no idea," Brad said, startling a chuckle from Kato. "If we miss it, we miss it. I was really just guesstimating the actual time of sunrise anyhow. More than anything, I couldn't watch you sleep any longer. I was feeling greedy to have your smiles." There was something in Brad's tone.

Kato stood still, taking in the moment. "Are you blushing?"

"No." The uncomfortably fast answer had Kato's cheeks aching as his smile grew bigger.

"Why don't I believe you?" He crawled onto the bed, chasing after Brad. "Come here. Let me feel those cheeks. I bet they're hot."

"No," Brad cried through his laughter, trying to scramble away. He wasn't quick enough. Kato snagged Brad around the waist and tucked Brad beneath him. He used his weight against Brad, pinning him to the bed.

"Come here. Those cheeks are mine. I bet they're red. Let me feel." With Brad's laughter ringing in his ears, Kato pressed several loud kisses to Brad's cheeks. "I knew it," he cried, making Brad laugh harder. "You're embarrassed." Kato gasped in mock horror. "Even after you agreed to no shame between us." He shook his head. All the wiggling and laughter beneath him had him rock hard. "I'm sorry, sexy. You've left me no choice. I'll have to spank you. Take your punishment with a smile."

Brad's hips lifted, openly teasing Kato. "No. Don't," Brad said in the fakest plea Kato had ever heard.

Kato ran his hand down Brad's body. "How will you ever learn if I let these things pass?" He shaped the outline of Brad's erection through his shorts.

Brad gasped. "You're right. I need to be punished."

The moment turned from playful to heated in a breath. "I'm sorry, baby. You're about to miss your sunrise."

Brad's hold tightened on Kato. "I feel like I'm already watching it."

Something shifted in Kato's chest. There was a flutter he couldn't define. They were going somewhere Kato had never been. He was excited and scared. Most of all, Kato couldn't think of a single thing he'd rather be doing or anyone he'd rather be with.

BRAD: *If you'd like, I could pick you up when you get off and keep you.*

Kato: *LOL! Did you just offer to keep me? Like a puppy?*

Brad: *Yep. I'll feed you and pet you. Take you to a groomer on occasion.*

Kato: *You're so deliciously weird.*

Brad: *Maybe. Is that a yes?*

Kato: *I'd love nothing more than to stay with you tonight.*

Brad: *Good. See you soon.*

FIVE

They fell into a pattern. Anytime Brad could, he was there the moment Kato got off work. Kato stayed the night. Brad took care of him. He loved it. In truth, it was Kato he loved. With every smile, silly text, and touch, Brad slipped a little further beneath Kato's spell. Sometimes, he scared even himself with how much he wanted this. A hundred times words had flown to Brad's lips—confessions, pleas, and vows. But the flashes of doubt and fear he'd seen in Kato's expression that first night on the beach still made an appearance occasionally, leaving Brad deflated. There was a part of Kato that Brad couldn't breach.

Tonight, those words were back, begging for release. With Kato in his space, shirtless and sexy,

Brad wanted to plead with Kato for every night to be like this one. Brad's lips stung. Kato nibbled on his bottom lip, refusing to deepen their kiss. Brad's mind was moments away from snapping. Kato had stolen his shirt and unzipped Brad's jeans, but he hadn't gone further. Instead, he'd spent the last half hour driving Brad insane with kisses.

"You should go wait for me in bed, preferably nude," Kato suggested. "I'll grab some water."

Brad didn't need to be told twice. "Okay." Even though he was in a hurry to have Kato, he didn't budge as Kato headed for the kitchen. Brad didn't want to miss a single moment of watching Kato cross the room. The way the muscles moved in his back and his round ass bounced when he walked kept Brad fascinated. His eyes refused to give up their feast. Only when Kato completely disappeared from sight did Brad push from the couch. He moved to kill the lights. Someone knocked on the door. Brad considered ignoring it. Kato had told him to go to bed. That's where Brad wanted to be. The only place Brad wanted to be. The knock sounded again, and Brad's shoulders fell. As he pulled the door open, Easton stepped inside—like he had no doubts over his welcome. Brad was too shocked to cut him off before he stood in the living room, looking in every direction. He was dressed to kill. Solid black long sleeve shirt, hugging every perfectly shaped line and black jeans that fit like a second skin. The dark shade perfectly highlighted his pale features, making his soulful green eyes stand out.

"Easton." He honestly had nothing else.

A sweet smile touched Easton's lips. "Hey, gorgeous."

Brad's stomach churned at the compliment. "What are you doing here?"

Easton's gaze slid down Brad's body, visibly eating up his lack of clothes. "Ever since I saw you a while back, I've been thinking—"

"I grabbed two bottles. After last night—"

"Oh, did you get a personal trainer?"

Kato drew up short, blinking in confusion. "Sorry. I didn't realize..."

Easton moved in Kato's direction. All Brad could do was watch in horror. Easton held his hand out for Kato to shake. Obviously, considering Kato couldn't see him, he didn't accept. "I'm not his personal trainer." The coldness in Kato's voice, coupled with his lack of handshake acceptance, had Easton dropping his hand and backing away.

Brad bit back an evil grin.

Easton shifted nervously. "Sorry. I just assumed.

You're in workout shorts and have water. Plus, you're..." he motioned toward Kato's hardened body, as if searching for the right words. "Never mind," he finished, sounding overly bright. "I just stopped by to see Brad, but I didn't realize he had company. So, I guess I'll come back another time." His gaze slid Brad's way. He looked at Brad's from beneath his lashes. "We'll talk."

Brad blinked in confusion, incapable of finding any words. Too many screams were vibrating off the walls of his mind. The loudest one yelled for Brad to tell him to get fucked and never come back. Brad's lips wouldn't budge. Instead, he dipped his chin, acknowledging Easton's claim. He watched as Easton let himself out. Even once he was gone, Brad couldn't move.

A sexy sounding chuckle caressed his ears. Brad's gaze shot to Kato. He was smiling. "Who was that?"

Brad blinked a few more times. "My ex."

Kato's smile slipped away. "The cheat?"

In Brad's shock, he nodded before he realized what he'd done and used his words. "Yeah. That one."

"Whoa."

"Yeah."

"Well," Kato said, sounding pragmatic. "That happened. Do you still want to go to bed or would you like to start drinking?"

A smile exploded across Brad's face. "As if I'd ever pass up going to bed with you."

Kato's expression turned heated. "You should lock the door. No more answering it tonight."

Brad turned the lock with no qualms. "Whatever you want, it's yours."

"Mhmm," Kato hummed. "I like that. Bed. Now."

Brad quickly moved to do as told. Easton was already forgotten. In fact, Kato had wiped Easton from Brad's mind weeks ago. He didn't have room for anyone else.

A HAPPY HAZE coated Kato's brain. It had been that way since he'd met Brad. The only way he could be happier was if Flynn would stop timing his flirting to coincide with Brad picking him up. He knew it was purposeful. There was no way he showed up at the exact time for Kato to leave each day by accident. Still, Brad hadn't bitched, and Kato was always so damn happy to be with Brad, Flynn was forgotten the moment Brad arrived. He wished that time of day wasn't still three hours away. Kato rubbed his chest. Damn. He was attached. There was no lying to himself. He was pretty certain Brad was the one. Kato took a breath. He didn't know where to go with that knowledge. The air thickened. Kato's mind drifted. He swore he could still feel the vibration of Brad's moans. Kato brushed his lips. He missed Brad's kiss.

"Do you have a minute?"

Kato straightened in his seat. "Sure. What's up?" Even though Detroit was his friend, he was still married to Kato's boss. He never, ever wanted Detroit to think Kato took advantage of his kindness. It was bad enough he was already such a burden on Detroit's time.

"There's someone up front requesting you give them a tour. Also, Janie called in. If you're interested, you can have her hours tonight. You'd just be sending people to their assigned playrooms."

Kato winced. "Damn. I wish I could say yes. You know I could use the money, but I already made plans with Brad."

"Oooh," Detroit said, his voice moving closer. "Brad again. Valentine's Day was like more than two months ago. You've seen him almost nightly since then. I'm sensing a serious relationship here."

To Kato's horror, heat rushed to his cheeks. He tried beating it back. "I thought I had a tour waiting."

"They'll wait." Detroit didn't sound concerned. "So, spill. Oh, wait. Has he met your parents? That's the real question here, because your dad…"

Yeah. Kato knew. His dad was… supportive in an unwilling way. Like he didn't interfere in Kato's life, but he also didn't keep his opinions to himself. "We have dinner plans." Kato dragged out each word, making sure Detroit understood exactly how worried he was over their upcoming plans. "Sunday night. I've put them off as long as I can, but Mom is getting restless. She threatened to track Brad down and take him to lunch alone. I can't have that."

Detroit sucked in a hiss. "She hates the age gap, doesn't she?"

Kato shook his head. "Oddly, she hasn't said anything about Brad's age. I think she's so damn thrilled he's a lawyer that he could be eighty and she'd be cool. But she thinks I'm hiding him—like I'm ashamed of my family."

"What does Brad say about meeting them?"

Kato shrugged. "Honestly, he's so laidback. I think he'd agree to anything I suggested. It's actually a bit terrifying—like I expect he'll explode one day, showing his true colors. Surely no one is so calm. Soothing."

"Awwww." Detroit's cooing had Kato blushing again. He stood. Detroit rushed to fix things. "No. I'm sorry. You're making me all happy and shit. Calm and soothing is perfect for you. And, honestly, I don't think it's an act. I don't know Brad extremely well, but—from what I do know—he never loses his cool. I think he's just one of those quiet on the inside people. He handles some pretty important multi-million-dollar shit. He has to be collected."

Kato cocked his head and thought it over. Everything Detroit said made sense. "That's true. I guess we'll see. So far, I have no complaints."

"Good. If anything comes up and you decide you want Janie's hours, just show up or call me. I'll come get you."

"Thanks." Kato really did appreciate it. He needed every penny he could get. It was important to him to be independent, but it was also expensive. He had a ton of doctor bills. Life was starting to crush him a little. Well, a lot, but Brad's presence in his life cushioned the blow.

"No worries. I left that guy who wants a tour at the front door. His name is Easton."

Kato's steps faltered. Wasn't that Brad's ex's name too? Kato shook it off. It wasn't a common name, but neither was it so unique there couldn't be two. He held tightly to hope all the way to the front door. Kato pasted on his brightest smile, praying it wasn't him.

"Easton? Are you ready to see the rest of the club?"

"It's you I'd like to see, but I understand that comes with a tour."

Kato's smile fell. He even recognized the voice, and he'd only heard it once. It was hard to forget fake nice coated in superiority. Even though it took everything he possessed, Kato forced the smile back to his lips. "Who knows? Once you see the place, you might decide you like it here after all. Follow me." Kato showed Easton his back. He didn't really care if he followed. "This first room is the public viewing area. It's a voyeur's dream, I'm told. Monday through Thursday, we have—"

"Did Brad tell you about me?" Easton asked, cutting him off.

Kato decided he'd give his tour and Easton could question him all he wanted. He wouldn't give the man any ammunition. "Alcohol cannot be served in the same establishment as people showing their naughty bits, so the Den of Payne is BYOB, but—rest assured—the bar carries plenty of mixers as well as nonalcoholic beverages."

"Did you meet Brad here?"

Kato stuck to his usual speech, skipping quite a bit of the sales pitch since Easton wasn't here for that anyhow. "Down the hall and to your left, the rooms are cozier. Half are reserved for exhibitionists. The other half gets to watch. To the right, you'll find private playrooms for the darker ta—"

"Brad is in charge of an entire law team. He's important. Do you have any idea what it would do to his reputation if his team learned what you do?"

Kato stopped pretending Easton cared about the club's amenities. "Brad is no longer your concern. He's mine."

"Brad will always be my concern. He planned to marry me, you know? He'd bought the ring and everything. My brother warned me just in time for me to put a stop to that nonsense."

"Sounds like he made a narrow escape. If you have no interest in a tour, I'll show you out. The owners here aren't fond of people coming to gawk and judge. This is a haven where people can be themselves."

Easton touched his arm. Kato took a step back

without thought. He didn't like being at a disadvantage. Easton could do anything, and Kato couldn't see it coming. The man didn't take the hint. "I know there's no reason for you to believe it, but I care about Brad. My brother works on his team. Everything Brad does reflects on his position. That includes who he chooses to spend his time with. He should be with someone with a future. Someone who doesn't embarrass him."

Kato couldn't hold back his sneer. "I suppose you think that he should be with you?"

"Maybe so," Easton said without an ounce of shame. "My parents are both respected attorneys. They sit on several boards. I can further his career. You can only tank it." Easton patted him. He was obviously a toucher. "Just think about it, okay? If you really care about Brad, you won't drag him down with you. He deserves better."

He felt the moment Easton left him alone. Easton's oppressive weight cleared from the air. Even with him gone, Kato still couldn't breathe. He wanted to call Brad right then, and laugh about his crazy ex. The old him would've done just that. The new Kato was insecure and lacking. This version didn't have anything to offer but debt and—as Easton had pointed out—a job that could ruin Brad's reputation. He didn't want to give Easton's claims credence. Kato wanted to forget this day happened. Unfortunately, his brain had already absorbed the blows and saw the truth. Brad was better off without a blind boyfriend who peddled sex. Kato would never be anything but a burden.

EVERYTHING FELT OFF TONIGHT. From the moment Brad picked Kato up from work, every kiss felt empty. Each touch, forced. Kato was quiet and restless. He kept moving to the kitchen and coming back empty handed. The moment Brad thought he was finally settled on the couch, Kato was back on his feet, pacing. Since he'd managed to sit still for a solid two minutes, Brad stroked the back of Kato's hand, hoping to soothe whatever ate at him. He needed to touch Kato, reassure himself they were okay. The moment Brad made contact with Kato's skin, Kato shot from the couch again.

Brad bit back the hurt. "Do you want to talk about it?"

Kato flashed him a brittle smile. "Detroit offered me an extra shift tonight. I'm just feeling torn. Stressing. I want to spend time with you, but I need the money. My bills keep piling up. But every time I decide I'll go in for a few hours, I think I'll be disappointing you. Sorry." Kato sat down again. He was back on his feet before Brad could form a sentence.

He couldn't stand this. "If you need to work, I don't mind taking you. I'll even stay with you if you're worried I'll feel neglected."

Kato's shoulders fell. "You hate it there."

Brad wished he could deny it. "Sorry. I'm just awkward and I feel old and out of place there. Sorry," Brad said again, because—when it came to this subject—Brad was failing Kato. "I only brought it up that one time. It hasn't occurred to me that I might be doing or saying something that makes you feel guilty for needing to work." Kato growled and scrubbed his hands through his hair at Brad's apology. A knot formed in Brad's gut. This was about more than Brad's dislike of Kato's job. He felt it. Brad checked his tone. "You can talk to me, Kato. About anything."

"I just need my job, you know? Things have been hard."

"If you need help, I'm here." Brad tried to pick his words carefully. He tried expressing himself without hurting Kato's pride. "I make good money.

More than I need. Plus, I'm boring and never do anything, so if you need anything, I don't mind covering you. You give me way more in exchange." He knew he was explaining himself badly, but there was no good way to approach the topic of money.

An ugly sounding snort escaped Kato. "Am I supposed to become your charity case now?"

"No," Brad argued. "That's not what I'm say—"

"Then what are you saying, Brad?" Kato asked, cutting him off. "It sounds a hell of a lot like you're offering to make me your whore."

Brad scrubbed his hands over his face. "Forget it. Do what you want. I was trying to tell you that I love you and want to take care of you, but you don't want either of those things, so fuck it. Go back to work. I shouldn't care, right? I mean, that's where I met you."

Kato exploded, shocking Brad with his instant rage. "Do you think this is what I want? Honestly? Do you think the biggest dream I had for myself was answering the phone at a BDSM club?"

"No, I—"

"I don't want to fucking hear anything you have to say," Kato yelled, cutting him off again as if he hadn't been asking questions. "I had a life once too. A future. Do you really believe that I want nothing more than to be here like this?" he spat, pointing at the floor.

Something shattered inside Brad. All the times he'd caught a glimpse of fear and unhappiness in Kato's expression came to a head. "You're right." Even to his ears, Brad sounded dead. "Why would you want to be right here with me?"

Kato's expression changed, snapping closed. "Brad, I—"

Brad stood. "No. I understand. Come on. I'll take you to work."

"Brad, I—"

"You said what you meant," Brad said, cutting him off. He didn't want to watch Kato backpedal. "You're unhappy. With everything. Including me."

"I'm not."

"You are." The laughter in Brad's tone had no humor tinting it. "It's okay. You're young. You have years and years to figure out what you want. I don't. I've wasted too much of my life on people who don't want the same things I do. You won't be content with me and I don't care to chase you. I want someone who wants to be with me. No games."

"Goddamn it. I'm not playing games," Kato growled.

Brad stared at Kato's open frustration and felt

nothing but empty. "Maybe not, but you don't want a quiet peaceful life together. I'm not sure you know what you want. All I know is, it's not me."

"What the fuck, Brad? All this is just because I need to work, and you don't like my job."

Brad shook his head. It didn't matter Kato couldn't see him. The denial was for him and everything he'd just lost. "All this is because you don't love me. No amount of pushing or pulling on my end will make you feel what you don't feel. I'm tired of watching you struggle with yourself, trying to force yourself to want this. Wasting another night won't change anything, so I'd rather not."

Kato's features hardened. "So, time with me is wasted time. Good to know."

"No," Brad said honestly. "Time with me is wasted time, and I can't take the thought of stealing any more from you." He headed for the door. After a moment, Kato followed him, looking defeated.

"For the record, I never felt like I was wasting my time with you. But you're right. You deserve someone else."

The words were a knife in Brad's already breaking heart. It was one tiny argument. That was all it had taken to destroy them. He wanted to apologize, but he couldn't go back to swallowing his love, because he feared Kato didn't want it. Now, he knew Kato didn't, and it was hell.

"You deserve the world," Brad told him honestly. Even he heard the pain in his voice. "Fuck." Brad had nothing else. Everything hurt too badly. He couldn't keep talking. If he did, he'd probably end up convincing Kato to stay in a relationship that made him miserable. Brad couldn't do that. He needed Kato to be happy even if that meant they never saw each other again.

SIX

Technically, Kato's shift had ended an hour earlier. Since he didn't have a way home, he wasn't in any hurry to leave. He could call a cab. Kato couldn't really afford that. Instead, he put file folders together, giving his hands something to do.

"Incoming message from Brad."

Kato's mind froze. His heart missed a beat. It had been two days. Two of the longest damn days of his life since he'd seen or heard from Brad. After Brad had booted him from his life, he'd taken Kato to work, ripped out his heart by kissing Kato goodbye, and left for good. Every second had been hell since.

"Play message from Brad."

"Brad: Hey, I just got a call from your mom. It

seems you never cancelled the dinner she planned for us."

"Fuck," Kato cursed, dragging out the word. He'd been so immersed in his misery, wallowing away, he'd forgotten all about dinner with his parents.

"I didn't have the heart to tell her we're no longer together. Nor do I think it's my place. So, I'll be there to pick you up in a few, and you can tell them whenever you're ready."

Kato dropped his forehead to the desk. "You're way too good for me." He should've told Brad that a long time ago. Now, he could only say it to an empty office.

"Before I get there, I have something I need to say, and I don't want to fight again. So, I'll say it here. I want you to be happy." Kato leaned back in his chair, closed his eyes, and listened to the sound of Brad's voice. He missed everything about Brad so fucking much. "Even if we're not together, I can live with anything as long as I know you're okay. Damn." Kato flinched. The curse sounded as if it was ripped from Brad's soul. It took Kato's breath. "You really are amazing. I'm fighting the urge to tell you how much I miss you. Instead, I'll say, I hope you find what you're missing and know I'll always cheer for you. Thank you for brightening my life for a little while. I know you'll set the world ablaze and find your happiness."

"Damn. You must be the biggest idiot I've ever met for letting that go."

Kato's eyes flew open at the sound of Flynn's voice. "Why are you eavesdropping?" Even to his ears, Kato sounded tired and bitter.

"It's not eavesdropping if your office door is standing wide open." His voice moved closer. "You can say I'm butting into something that's none of my business. That'll be fair, because I don't intend to take back my opinion. You're a fucking fool."

"You don't know anything about me or this." Kato felt for the paperclip on his file, going back to work. He had a system of paperclip placement that let him know which drawer the file belonged in.

"I've heard and seen enough to muddle my way through," Flynn said, his voice moving closer. He obviously had no intentions of leaving. "You lost a good one."

An ugly sounding snort escaped Kato. "Yeah, and every time he came here, he found you, trying your damnedest to fuck me. Why should he stick around?" Kato was desperate for someone else to take the blame. He couldn't stand the hurt.

"Don't put this on me, my heart. I can't come

between people where there's no space. My guess is, he just wanted you to do or say something to prove that space doesn't exist. You're sexy." Flynn dropped the compliment like it was the truth and not praise. "Wherever you go, you'll have someone flirting with you. There's nothing for it. That's why you make sure to use your words so your at-home kitten knows his worth." Kato heard the wheels move on the chair across from his desk. It was obvious Flynn intended to settle in for a chat. "You see, I'm really good at reading people. I have to be to do this job. Your man might be submissive in bed, but he's not like that dude out there who likes it when people literally walk all over him. If you want your man to sit, stay, and purr happily, you need to learn when to wield your dominance and when to abstain. You need to learn to bend where it matters, or you will lose him for good." Flynn didn't let up or give outrage time to grow. "Also, you need to stop living the bullshit sayings that are crocheted on pillows. Trust isn't freely given until lost. You have to work for it. Every day. Especially with someone who's still obviously licking their wounds."

"Do you have some sort of cat fetish? That's like the third cat analogy you've used."

Flynn made a dismissive sound. "I like furry

things. It doesn't matter. The point is, I can tell by the way you light up when he's around that you feel something for him. So, don't be stupid. No more pillow crochet living. You don't have to love yourself before you love others. Just love him. That's all he needs. Stop thinking you need to be more before you use your goddamn words."

"You should stop flirting with me then." Even Kato was surprised by not only his words but the forcefulness of them. This seemed the place to start if Kato hoped to win back Brad.

"Yeah," Flynn said, dragging out the word. "That's probably not going to happen. This is who I am. But don't take me to heart. It's all in fun. If I was truly determined to have you, I already would have done so."

"Are you ready to go?"

Goddamn it. Every fucking time. It was like Flynn and Brad called each other ahead of time each day and arranged a time to meet. Worse than that, today Brad didn't sound angry. It was like he'd conceded to Flynn.

Kato pushed to his feet. "Yes. Sorry. I should've called and cancelled dinner. I completely forgot."

"It's fine. Good to see you again, Flynn." He was

so formal. It was a punch to Kato's gut—like they were strangers.

"You too," Flynn said, moving ahead of Kato to the door. "You're looking as sexy as always." A spurt of jealousy clawed at Kato's throat. Flynn didn't stop. "When can we expect you to become a full member? I offer services you might find... freeing."

"My knees are too bad for this place. Kato, we're running behind." Brad couldn't have sounded any less interested if he tried.

Pride swelled in Kato's chest. It disappeared every bit as quickly. Brad didn't belong to him. Not anymore. He'd fucked that up. Still, without thought, he reached for Brad's hand. Kato caught himself at the last second. It was too late. As always, Brad didn't fail him. He tucked Kato's hand in the crook of his arm like he did every day, as if nothing had changed.

"Do you need to tell Detroit you're leaving?"

"I'll send him a message later." Kato didn't want to risk giving up Brad's arm and losing it. This might be the last time Brad let him touch him. "Again, I'm so sorry. You know how things just slip away from me sometimes."

"It's fine," Brad said, maneuvering Kato through the building. "I didn't have any other plans tonight."

Fear choked Kato. Brad didn't have plans

tonight. Did he have plans for a different night? Had he been replaced by Easton already? Brad could have anyone. He was sexy and successful. Anyone would be damn lucky to have him. Kato was no one with nothing to offer. He was a burden. Brad could be holding someone else the second he left Kato. He could be on his knees for someone else.

"Stop."

Kato immediately froze, expecting to trip.

"Sorry," Brad said, sounding tired. He urged Kato to keep walking. "I should've considered my words. I didn't mean stop moving. Stop thinking whatever you're thinking before you bruise me."

Brad's claim made Kato realize how tightly he held Brad's arm in the throes of his inner panic. "Jesus. I'm sorry."

"It's okay," Brad said quietly. "You do it all the time without thought. That's how I knew you were miserable with me."

Everything inside Kato deflated. He wanted to scream. No matter how he fought for the right words, he couldn't find them. He didn't know how to make Brad understand. There had never been anything wrong with Brad or them. It was Kato. Everything was wrong with him, except Brad. Well, now he could include Brad since he'd fucked them up the way he did everything. Kato wasn't surprised. He always lost the things he loved the most.

THEY MADE the drive to Kato's parents' house in complete silence. It was uncomfortable and heavy. Choking. Brad didn't know why he hadn't demanded Kato cancel this dinner. It made no sense for him to be here, except that he loved Kato. If Kato canceled this meal and told his parents they were over, then they were done. After two nights without Kato and forty-eight hours to think, he wasn't as sure he was finished with this. Brad had combed through every second they'd spent together and decided something was wrong, but not with them. They'd been perfect until one moment they weren't. He had no fucking clue why. It was like an entire falling out happened between them while he wasn't there. Until he understood why they were over, Brad couldn't accept they were.

Brad parked at the curb in front of a modest home with light yellow siding. From the outside, it looked to be a four or five-bedroom house. The large front lawn was immaculate. There was an abandoned football in the yard and chain-link fence around the backyard. He spotted a wooden play set out back. For a moment, he sat there staring. Kato had grown up here. It looked like a nice, normal neighborhood. He wondered if Kato had played in the streets with his friends or tossed a football around with his dad. There were dozens of questions he could still ask Kato about his life. How could they be through?

"I can go inside alone. You can drive away and never think of me again."

At Kato's offer, Brad's gaze shifted his way. He looked resigned and sad—like he expected Brad would leap at the chance. "You're not getting rid of me." Without expounding, Brad jumped from the car and circled around to collect Kato. After helping Kato from the car, Brad tucked the man's hand in the crook of his arm and headed for the house. "I could picture you here. Did you have a lot of neighborhood friends growing up?"

A smile brightened Kato's face. "We ran all over the neighborhood. Detroit's parents live four streets over. They're terrible people, but he used to sneak out, and we'd walk to the store. We'd buy candy and drinks then hide out in this little patch of woods a block away. Sometimes, I miss being young."

The confession surprised a laugh from Brad. "You're still young."

"Am I?" Kato asked the question as if genuinely inquiring.

Brad pulled Kato to a stop before they made it to the door. He needed to say a few things before they were under the watchful gazes of Kato's parents. "You're young and beautiful—inside and out. Losing the ability to see yourself in a mirror didn't change your reflection. You said you once had dreams for yourself. They're still there, waiting for you to come for them. Anytime you stop seeing yourself as the amazing person you are, call me, and I'll remind you." Without waiting for Kato to argue, Brad headed for the door. It opened before he could knock.

Kato's mom, Megan was all smiles as she let them in. "It's so good to finally meet you. Of course, we talk so much on the phone, I feel like I already know you." It was true. Megan had called his office once, in a panic, because Kato wasn't answering his phone. Since Kato's phone had been dead, Brad had given her all his numbers. She hadn't stopped calling since. He liked her.

Brad was forced to only one arm hug her since Kato wasn't giving up his other arm. "It's good to see you, Megan." His gaze moved away from the woman who looked so much like Kato and landed on the man standing beside her.

The dark-haired guy held out his hand. "Scott."

Brad shook his hand. "Brad."

Megan spoke up, stealing his focus again. "It'll be another fifteen minutes on the lasagna. I had to take Brandon to soccer practice, so I'm running behind."

"That's fine." He wasn't in a hurry. Brad was hyper aware it might be his last chance to spend any time with Kato. He wouldn't rush the day away.

"Why don't you come with me?" Scott said, motioning toward the garage. "I'd love to get a second opinion on why this old truck won't start."

"Um."

Kato squeezed his arm as if reassuring him.

Brad tossed a look his way. Kato was smiling. Damn it. "Sure." Even Brad heard the reluctance in his voice. Kato gave his ass a pat as he walked away. Brad bit back a sigh. This entire situation was uncomfortable as hell. They felt like they were still together. It hurt. Not to mention, Scott was maybe five years older than him, but he was Kato's dad. He wasn't sure how to act. As the door to the kitchen closed behind him, Brad decided to be a little forthright. "I have to be honest, I really don't know anything about cars."

A bark of laughter escaped Scott. He glanced over his shoulder at Brad. "Me either."

Brad eyed the older model Chevy truck sitting nearby with its hood up. "Okay."

Scott reached inside the truck and came out with two beers. He passed one Brad's way. His smile was a bit sheepish. "My only hope is that we never break down on the side of the road. I don't want to have to explain that I know nothing about car mechanics and never do anything but sit out here and drink." A chuckle escaped Brad as he popped the tab on the can. Scott took a swig of his beer before continuing. He motioned toward where they'd left Kato and Megan behind. "They'll want time to gush over you and it's my job to give them that time. It's our job to drink while I pretend to threaten to break your kneecaps if you ever hurt my son, which—honestly— is a speech I'd never thought I'd have to give when I had all sons. So, you're a lawyer," Scott tacked on before Brad was forced to find some response to Scott's speech.

Brad nodded. "I'm in charge of the legal department at Green's Fighter Fuel and act as the owners' personal attorney."

"You're a rich man's lackey."

"Rich men pay the best," Brad said without an ounce of shame.

Scott nodded. He looked unfazed. "How did you meet Kato?"

Even though it was obvious Scott was only making awkward conversation to fill the silence, Brad choked on his beer. Scott laughed as Brad coughed before slapping him across the back.

"Don't worry. I already know you met at that weirdo club where he works. He told us the story. It's funny how life turns out." Scott sipped his beer, getting philosophical while Brad regained his breath. "I teach marketing at Pebble Lake High. Detroit was in my class for two years. I always knew he was a strange kid, but I didn't try to stop Kato from being friends with him like a lot of the parents did. Hell, it wasn't really necessary. Detroit's parents never let him do anything unless it was school or sports. Well," Scott mused, staring off into space as if seeing the past. "They always let him go home with that Micah kid." Scott shook his head. "Anyhow, Detroit was the only who showed up after Kato..." Scott seemed to struggle for words. Brad held his silence, waiting. Scott cleared his throat. "He was the only who showed up. I mean, at first a lot of people came around, but Detroit was the only one who really showed up, you know?" Scott's gaze locked onto Brad at the question. Brad nodded, since it seemed Scott looked for a response. He gave Brad a sharp nod. "You see a lot shit happen to kids that should never happen to kids when you teach as long as I have. Still, I'm glad I never told Kato to steer clear of Detroit. That's why I also chose to keep my mouth shut about him working in that club, and I won't say anything now about this huge age gap thing, or how you two met." He looked tired and serious. Brad sympathized. He wasn't giving up Kato, but he understood. Brad froze at the thought. He meant it. He wasn't giving up Kato or them. Scott shook his head. "I just hope I'm telling another story in a few years about how I kept my mouth shut about you and it was the best decision I ever made."

Damn. That was the nicest not keeping his nose out of it speech Brad could have hoped to receive. Brad polished off his beer. "I hope so too."

Scott accepted his empty can and hid the evidence under a bag in the trashcan. He flashed Brad a conspiratorial smile. "She's not an idiot, but we like to keep up pretenses."

They seemed like a nice couple. "Do you think we're safe to go back inside, or are they still gushing?"

Scott eyed the door. "We should probably have one more just to be safe."

A chuckle escaped Brad. He didn't think the day would be too bad after all. Brad was still ready to be alone with Kato. They had things to discuss, but he could wait. Kato wanted Brad to know his family. Brad was learning there wasn't much he wouldn't do to make Kato happy.

———

WITH HIS EYES CLOSED, Kato focused on the way Brad toyed with his fingers. Since leaving his parents' house, Brad had been quiet. It wasn't an angry or heavy silence, so Kato chose to savor Brad's touch. This might be the last time. A smile tugged at his lips as Brad stroked his palm, drawing circles with his fingertip.

"Are you falling asleep?"

Kato's smile grew at the question. "Your voice is sexy. I don't think I've told you that." His throat swelled, catching him off guard. "I should have told you that."

"I love you." Brad didn't give Kato time to respond. "That's where I should have stopped talking the other night. I shouldn't have said the hundred other things you didn't deserve. I don't give a damn where you work. In fact, I don't understand why that came up at all."

"I told Flynn to stop flirting with me. That's the conversation you walked in on today. He said it probably wouldn't happen," Kato felt moved to add. "But I tried, and I'll keep trying. Also, you're right. I'm unhappy." It hurt more than Kato expected to admit to such a thing, but he was, and it wasn't fair to Brad for him to pretend otherwise. "My discontent has nothing to do with you or us. It's me. I wanted more from life than this. There's nothing wrong with my job, except it's a pity job. Payne doesn't need me. He could literally buy an answering machine to replace me." Once the flood gates opened, Kato couldn't stop. He knew he could talk to Brad. It felt good. "In fact, I'm pretty sure that's how the position was handled before I came along. I'm a burden." Once the confession was out there, hanging in the universe, Kato's admissions came faster, making him feel like he couldn't breathe. "I love you. I don't want to be a stone around your neck, dragging you down. You deserve better, but I can't quit. For fuck's sake, why did you even speak to me that first night?" The air thinned in the car. He tried filling his lungs without luck. "No matter what, I'll lose you. Either you'll get tired of my neediness or you'll get sick of Flynn's flirting. Then what? Do I quit my job and wait for you to resent me or do I stay and wait for you to hate me when I ruin your reputation?" In his panic, Kato didn't realize the car had stopped moving until he heard Brad's door slam. His door opened, and Brad was there, calming the storm, the way he always did.

"Breathe, baby," Brad said, his voice soothing away the panic. He held Kato against his chest. His steady heartbeat kissed Kato's ear.

Kato breathed.

"It's okay. I've got you. Stop thinking for a moment and listen to my voice."

Kato cleared his head. He thought of nothing more than the air entering and leaving his lungs. His heart slowed.

"Don't start thinking yet, okay? Just listen. I was so goddamn lonely when I met you. That's me admitting the worst thing possible. I'm independent and proud. I don't like anyone thinking I'm pitiful, but I was lonely. My house was silent as a church on Tuesday morning. But I would happily live that way forever if the alternative was being with someone who makes me feel used, unloved, and angry. I've lived that life. It's awful. You aren't that person. I want to help. Not because you're needy or I pity you. I want to help because I love you and your smile means everything. Please let me help."

Although he tried not to think, Brad fed him worries to consider. The panic tried racing back in. "I don't even know where to start. I feel useless and helpless *and are we sitting on the side of the road*?" Kato asked, hearing his horror as a loud truck passed.

"Yes." Brad sounded calm. Steady. He was so fucking perfect in every way. "You started hyperventilating. I didn't have time to go anywhere else. Fuck pride for a second, Kato. Let me do this for you. For us," he added quietly, stealing any hope of Kato saying no.

Everything Flynn said earlier slapped Kato in the face. He had to learn when to bend, or he would lose this amazing man.

"Easton said I would ruin you. I love you, Brad. I don't want to destroy you like I do everything else."

Brad's entire body tensed. "When did Easton say that?"

Kato petted Brad. He couldn't stop. This was the love of his life. He couldn't lose him. "Two days ago. He showed up at work. I didn't think about how my job would make you look at yours. When you said you didn't like me working there, it never occurred to me that you were worried what people would think."

"I don't give a damn what anyone thinks." The growl in Brad's voice had Kato pulling away. He had a bad feeling he was getting ready to see the explosion of temper he'd feared Brad hid. Brad went completely silent. If not for the light hold on his arms, Kato would've thought Brad disappeared. The quiet was unnerving. Kato couldn't take it.

"Are you okay?"

Brad cleared his throat. "I'm trying to decide if I'm enraged that Easton almost managed to ruin my life a second time, or if I'm relieved to finally know why you seem so unhappy sometimes." Brad drew an unsteady sounding breath. "I love you."

"I love you too." Kato needed Brad's happiness back. The past few days had been horrible. Everything he'd thought was getting better was suddenly worse. He hadn't felt so overwhelmed by life in a while.

Brad stroked Kato's forearms. His fingertips brushed back and forth, soothing Kato. "Listen, okay?"

Kato nodded. Whatever Brad needed, it was his.

"No one at my job gives any shits what I do when I go home. They're all just trying to get home to their lives. I'm not ladder climbing. The job I have is the one I want, and I'll likely stay there until I can't work another day. Even if all that wasn't true, nothing is more important to me than us. I'm not embarrassed by you or your job. You're mine. You're all I need and want." Kato kept nodding along and hanging on every word. "If you want to stay at the Den of Payne, that's fine. If you want to find a way to go back to school, I will help you in every way. I will find that path for you. It's completely your choice. I promise you the world is open to you. This isn't charity. We are a team. We're going home and you're moving in with me."

"But do you—"

"You're moving in with me," Brad said again over the top of him. "Are you happy with me? Be completely honest with no care of my feelings."

They needed this conversation. Brad deserved his honesty. Kato would die if he didn't talk to someone who wouldn't judge him. "You're the only thing that makes me happy. Everything else is shit. I never meant to make you feel like you're lacking in some way. You're not. We're not. I'm just not adjusting to this disability as well as I wish I could."

"That's understandable, baby. I don't know that I

could handle what you have. I've got you though. We'll do this together. Okay?"

Kato took his first real breath in a long time. "Okay."

"From now on, don't ever be afraid to talk to me. Okay?"

"Okay." Kato promised himself it was true. He wouldn't let his silence come between them.

"If Easton ever comes at you again, call me immediately. I plan to take care of that, but until then, I need to know you won't let him hurt us."

Kato nodded. "I should've talked to you right away. It's just that everything he said sounded convincing at the time on top of my insecurities. I won't let it happen again."

Brad stroked his face. Kato turned his head and kissed his hand. "It's my fault," Brad said, taking Kato by surprise. "If I'd spent every day telling you how amazing you are, you wouldn't have believed Easton. I was scared to show too much of my heart. I didn't want you to break it."

Kato couldn't take the sad note to Brad's voice. The thought of hurting Brad was a dagger in his heart. He felt like someone was sitting on his chest. "Come here," Kato begged, urging Brad closer. "You can trust me with everything," Kato swore as he lured Brad in for a kiss. As their lips met, peace settled over Kato. It would be okay as long as they were together. Kato would make sure of it. He loved Brad too much to fail him again.

FOR HOURS BRAD and Kato did nothing except hold each other. Half of Brad's body was asleep. He couldn't bring himself to care. With Kato's head on his chest and Kato's hand buried beneath his shirt, Brad was happy as hell. The sight of his bedroom ceiling wasn't boring him at all. Each time Kato lightly kissed his chest Brad felt another stitch tighten, tying his soul to Kato's.

"You can turn on the TV if you're bored. I won't be offended."

Brad tightened his hold on Kato at Kato's offer. "I'm good. There's nothing I'd rather be doing."

Kato's hand slipped down Brad's stomach. His fingers curled around the edge of Brad's waistband. "Nothing? Are you sure?" He worked the button loose on Brad's jeans and slowly slid down the zipper. "I think I can find something you'd like more."

Even as Brad's cock stirred, he covered Kato's

hand, stopping him. "You don't have to. I'm happy just being with you. Almost losing you was like my worst nightmare coming true. I'd never want you to think we're only about the sex."

Kato's tilted his chin up, giving Brad a clear look at his expression. He looked happy and in love. Brad's breath caught in his throat. He loved everything about Kato, from his gorgeous blue eyes to his even more beautiful spirit. Kato shook off Brad's hand and continued working to set Brad's erection free. "I know we're not about the sex. It's the fact that we're so damn beautiful together that makes the sex ten times better than anyone else would be. Not that you'll ever get to compare me to anyone." His fingers encircled Brad's erection. He stroked, stealing Brad's breath. "You should strip and ride me." Kato rolled toward the bedside table, freeing Brad to do as he suggested while digging out the lube. Brad shimmied out of his clothes while Kato did the same. He couldn't look away as Kato bared every inch of his tight body. Brad's stomach muscles clenched with lust.

The instant he was nude, Kato stretched out and coated his cock with lube. Brad never turned his gaze away. Kato looked sexy as fuck with his dick shiny and waiting. Brad crawled toward him, letting his hunger grow. Kato's face was hard. Until Brad straddled his hips. His features softened as his hands found the globes of Brad's ass. He always kept his face tilted toward Brad as if he could see.

Brad couldn't stop his tongue. He wanted to know every detail about Kato. "You always look like you're completely focused on me. Your eyes follow me even though I know you can't see me."

"I see shadows when the lights are bright," Kato said, explaining why his eyes still knew where to look. "But even when they're not, I feel you. It's like your energy is stronger than everything else in the room, even with other people around. Like tonight, at my parents' house, I could tell when you were in the room and exactly how far away you were. You're mine. I can pick you out of a crowd by the way you make me feel." He dragged Brad closer, positioning Brad over his dick. "Right now, I really want to be connected to you in every way. I want to feel that you still belong to me."

Brad lowered himself onto Kato's cock. He held his breath as Kato's dick stretched him and filled him. It wasn't until Kato was buried to the hilt that Brad released his breath. "You're the only person who's ever owned me. You're the only one who ever will."

Kato looked sexy as fuck with a flush riding high on his cheekbones and his lips parted on a pant. "You should kiss me."

Brad fell forward, bracing his weight on his palms on either side of Kato's head. As their lips met, Kato reached between them and massaged Brad's erection. Brad rocked, fucking Kato's hand and riding Kato's dick. Their tongues stroked and retreated, playing as their bodies strained. Kato didn't take mercy on him. He used both hands against Brad. He toyed with Brad's balls and fisted his cock, leaving Brad no choice but to abandon their kiss. On his knees, he ground down on Kato's erection, pulling pants and moans from Kato. Kato pumped at Brad's dick, driving Brad insane.

"That's it, sexy. Fuck me. Take what you want."

Brad fought for oxygen while Kato rambled.

"Damn, baby. You're so fucking beautiful on my dick. I swear I can almost see you when you're like this. That's how much you make me feel. Give me your cum. I want it," Kato demanded. His movements turned frantic. He stroked Brad so fast that Brad couldn't keep up. All he could do was hang on and keep a steady pace on Kato's cock. He changed angles, forcing Kato's dick to massage him internally in just the right spot. Brad closed his eyes and let the pressure build. Part of him wanted to stay on edge forever. The rest of Brad needed release.

"Fuck," Brad breathed, reaching for more. "You feel so good inside me. Let's do this forever."

"I love you, beautiful. You already know it's forever."

At Kato's promise, ecstasy slammed into Brad. The air left his lungs in a whoosh as he flew over the edge. Kato kept pumping, pulling every last drop of cum from Brad. He held still letting his orgasm do the work. His ass tried sucking Kato deeper. Guttural sounds and curses escaped Kato as he came. Brad watched every second. He couldn't tear his gaze away. The memory seared into his brain. They were beautiful together. It was like Brad caught a glimpse of a greater plan. The night they'd met, he'd gone some place he never would've gone for reasons he couldn't explain. That unusual decision had led to meeting this amazing man he wouldn't have met otherwise. It was supposed to happen. There was no other explanation for how he'd ended up here. No one could convince Brad otherwise. They would be okay because they were meant to be. Unexpectedly, tears filled Brad's eyes.

"I love you."

At Kato's claim, Brad sucked in a breath. He'd found his other half. "I love you too."

Kato lured him in for a kiss. As their lips met, Brad recognized the promise in their touch. This was forever. He wasn't stupid enough to ever doubt again.

SEVEN

"Are you still fighting with that thing?"

Kato stopped glaring at the computer he couldn't see at Detroit's interruption. "Microphone off," he said, because he'd actually remembered this time. "I'm getting better. Maybe." He laughed at his own aggravation. Brad had bought him a voice control system for his computer, making it possible for him to type, control his computer, surf the web, and—most importantly—attend online college courses. All of which Brad footed the bill. That last point didn't sit well with Kato. He was slowly learning to deal though because—as Brad had pointed out—they were a team. "Brad's been working with me every night. Together, we've managed to get me trained on this thing... mostly."

The chair squeaked as Detroit sat across from him. "Every time I think about giving him that two-day pass on a whim, I'm so goddamn thankful I did. He's made you smile again. I know you tried to pretend for a while, hoping no one would think you're weak, but he's brought the real you back. I'm so damn glad to see you again."

Kato nodded while swallowing back the pain of who he'd become before Brad. No doubt about it, Detroit giving Brad that pass had changed Kato's life. "He's amazing."

"He's also here."

Kato perked up at Detroit's claim. "Really?"

A soft chuckle sounded from Detroit's side of the desk. "There's more. I'm not sure if you're ready for the rest."

"What?" Even Kato heard the suspicion tinting that one word.

Thankfully, Detroit didn't leave him hanging long. "He took out a membership."

"What?" Kato's tone transformed from suspicion to anger without warning. Brad didn't need this place. He had Kato to ensure his every kink was satisfied.

Detroit rushed to smooth things over. "I tried to

tell him that he didn't need a membership if he wanted to hang out with you while you work, but he insisted. He said he wasn't ashamed to be a member here or for you to work here, and he felt the best way to show that was to pay the monthly dues."

Kato was somewhat appeased. "He didn't need to spend a bunch of money to make a point."

"I did if I want to play with you on the playroom floor."

Everything inside Kato lit like a wildfire at the sound of Brad's voice. "Hey, baby." Even to Kato's ears he sounded breathless. Damn. It was like Brad brought the sunlight.

"I'm letting you off early today," Detroit said, cutting in. "A private party has booked the club for the remainder of the day."

Kato felt his brow furrow. "I don't think that's happened the entire time I've worked here. Who booked the club?"

"John Green," Brad answered for Detroit. "My boss, John, has plans for his husband. Detroit has agreed to let me keep you today since I have to be here for this. Even though John booked the place under his name, I have to make sure he doesn't end up sued since people from work are also here."

That was all the explanation Kato needed to fly to his feet. If Brad had to be here, he'd be here with Kato. Brad was his. No one entertained him but Kato.

"There's no rush," Brad said moving closer. "They're setting up and I think this is the first time I've shown up and Flynn wasn't here."

Detroit cleared his throat. "Um, I think I'll just leave you two alone. I'll also close this," he added with a laugh. Kato heard the door click closed.

They were alone and shut away. That was Kato's favorite way to be with Brad. "You should probably lock that door before Flynn finds out you're here."

"True," Brad agreed.

Kato stood still and waited. "You know, I think it's you Flynn crushes on. I'm just the excuse he uses to be here every time you're here."

Brad invaded his space. Kato felt the heat of his skin a half second before Brad's hands slid across his waist. He drew Kato closer. "It doesn't matter. You're the only one for me. I don't know why I can't go a few hours without missing you. All day I've waited for this." Brad's lips touched the corner of Kato's mouth. Kato turned his head and chased Brad's kiss. He completely understood Brad's point. It had only been a few short hours since Brad dropped him off at work and Kato felt the absence all the way to his soul. Their lips met. Brad's teeth sank into Kato's bottom lip. His world felt right again.

Kato caressed Brad's chest as they tasted each other. He never got enough of feeling Brad's steady heartbeat. Before Brad, Kato hadn't realized how simply knowing someone existed could be so important. Kato was stupid in love with this man who'd taken over his life. The places he'd felt the weakest, Brad had invaded and shored up, making him feel strong again. When he'd lost his sight, he'd stopped seeing a future. Brad had given it back. Kato had to do everything in his power to hang on to him.

"How long do you think we have until someone comes looking for us?"

As Brad stole another kiss, he growled against Kato's lips. "Probably not long enough to ensure you never step into this office again without thinking of me."

Kato chuckled as he chased after Brad's lips. "That's already the case everywhere I go." He fingered Brad's soft Henley. "Is this the shirt I bought you? Detroit promised me it matches your eyes."

"It is. I didn't think there was any sense in doing

the three-piece suit thing since I won't be in the office today. Plus, I just love wearing this shirt. It always makes me think of you."

Kato bit his bottom lip, fighting a smile. Brad made huge purchases and massive gestures for Kato all the time. Yet, he always made Kato feel like the little things Kato could do for him in exchange we're just as big. Today, Kato intended to do his best to even the score a little. It was his turn to do something special for the man who'd given him the world. Kato traced Brad's lips with his fingertips before stroking the man's nose. He loved memorizing Brad's features. Brad was beautiful. "I've been fighting with the computer today."

Brad moved Kato's fingertips to his lips, so he could kiss them. "Are you having any luck?"

"Actually, yes. I made it through two classes. Turned in a homework assignment and got some stuff printed off without any help."

"You've been very productive." Kato could hear the smile in Brad's voice. "Did you learn anything new?"

Kato nodded. "Detroit tells me this extremely sexy man applied for membership today. I'm thinking about seducing him into joining me in one of the private playrooms someday."

"What's his name? I'll have him killed."

Happiness had Kato laughing out loud. "I love you."

"I love you too," Brad said, returning the words just as quickly, the way he always did. Kato felt the air change. Brad turned serious. His hold tightened on Kato. "You're my best friend. I can't imagine life without you."

Kato's throat tightened. "Same," he choked out, feeling the words all the way to his bones.

A knock sounded from the hallway. "All right, guys. Get dressed and join your friends."

"Sigh. We've been summoned," Brad said in mock disappointment. "I guess I have to share you sometimes."

A nervous flutter ran through Kato. "It seems so. Lead the way." Kato measured every breath as Brad took his hand and headed out. As they traversed the hallway, Kato wondered if he would be sick or hyperventilate. He hadn't expected to be this scared. Brad came to a sudden stop. Kato molded against his back and dropped his lips to Brad's shoulder, waiting.

"Um, why are your parents here?"

Kato didn't respond. He was too busy trying not

to faint. The building was completely silent—like everyone collectively held their breath.

"All my family is here too," Brad whispered over his shoulder, pulling a laugh from Kato. Kato turned Brad in his arms. He pushed all fear aside and dropped to one knee. Whistles filled the air.

"Bradley Lee Hollister, this is where we met. This place will always be the spot where my life took its greatest turn and fate showed its hand. I can't think of a better place to ask, will you marry me?"

Nothing. Dead silence.

The backs of Kato's eyes stung. He swore he could feel Brad's shock. "I wish I could see your face right now."

Brad took his hands and urged Kato to his feet as he led Kato's hands to his face. "You can see my face in your own way." Brad's cheeks were wet. "I love you. I'd be proud to be your husband." The cheers and catcalls were deafening. Brad kept kissing him and babbling between kisses. "Oh my god. I love you so much. How did you do all this? When did you have time?"

"With the computer you bought me, I started tracking people down. Your mom helped, and John obviously. He surprised me with how willing he was to set you up to believe he'd booked the place for the night. Don't worry. Your parents think this is just a regular nightclub."

Brad kissed him again. He hadn't let go of Kato's face yet. "I'm not worried over that. My mom stripped to pay her way through college. That's where she met my dad. They don't care about this place."

A surprised bark of laughter escaped Kato. Brad never stopped surprising him with little details of his life. He'd won the fucking lottery when he'd met Brad. Everything about himself that Kato had doubted and hated, Brad had cherished until he flourished. Kato didn't doubt for a single moment their life together would be beautiful.

"Champagne and toasts," John yelled, pulling them from their bubble. Kato turned to join the people who would become their extended family. The ones who'd shown up as proof they believed in Kato and Brad too. It wasn't them against the world— like a lot of couples. They were soulmates who'd been forced to their knees, so they could find one another. They were each other's saviors. Each other's port in the storm. Together, they were beautiful.

FLYNN TOOK his champagne to the front foyer where he could escape the noise. Even though he worked in a club, he didn't care for crowds. Not to mention, most of his work was done one on one. The tiny area between the front entrance and the public playroom was normally used to keep anyone without a membership from seeing anything they shouldn't. It's where guests waited for tours and packages were delivered. Tonight, it was the perfect place to escape the overly happy crowd, celebrating Kato and Brad. He was truly overjoyed for the pair. What they found together was rare whether they realized it or not. People found love every day, but more often than not it was the temporary kind. It only took one look at Kato and Brad to see theirs was not. They would grow old together. It was... sweet.

Flynn closed his eyes and inhaled, soaking up the silence. Sometimes, he missed Plockton. The small town in the highlands of Scotland didn't hold much interest for him any longer. There was no family waiting for him to visit. In fact, there was nothing there at all but a beautiful loch and silence. Still, he did miss the peace at times. Loud banging on the front door had Flynn's eyes snapping open. "What the fook is all this?" Flynn's accent thickened in his annoyance. "Oy. The place is shut you feckin idiot."

Flynn ripped open the door not bothering to hide his rage.

A tiny blond male with flashing green eyes stared back at Flynn with an equal amount of irritation. "Where's Kato?"

Flynn leaned his hip into the doorframe and kept the path blocked. "I imagine he's off celebrating his engagement to that sexy lawyer." The irritation turned to full-on fury in the sprite's eyes. Flynn bit back his laughter. He knew exactly who he was dealing with. Flynn had been standing less than three away when Brad's ex had gotten high and mighty with Kato, trying to work his way back into Brad's life. More likely, his wallet, but whatever. He'd tried to hurt Kato. Flynn wasn't someone people crossed.

"Where might he be celebrating?"

Flynn lifted one shoulder in a half shrug. "That's none of my business, now is it?"

Easton pulled himself up to his full five-eight stance, which still made Flynn's neck hurt looking down at him. "Everyone in this club is about to care after I drag it through the court. Someone gave channel twelve surveillance footage of me entering this place. Since my mom is currently running for governor, it's been blasted all over the news for the past two hours, damaging my family and my reputation. Kato is the only who could've done it."

A smirk pulled at Flynn's lips. "Well, A, we don't have surveillance. That would be a violation of extreme privacy around here. B, the only camera that could've caught you entering this place is on the pole behind you. That's belongs to the county, so Kato wouldn't have access to it. And, C, it would be interesting as hell to watch Kato sift through video footage to find a clip of you, being as how he's blind."

"What?"

That was what Flynn thought. It wasn't easy to tell Kato couldn't see. He rarely went anywhere he hadn't memorized his way around. Not to mention, he could still focus on outlines. People seldom realized he was blind unless Kato told them.

Flynn's smirk became a full-blown smile at Easton's surprise. He nodded. "He's blind. It's pretty easy to substantiate, considering his injury was heavily publicized in Washington." Easton's brow furrowed, and Flynn straightened away from the doorway. "You should probably march your enraged arse down to the county building and find out who leaked that tape. It didn't happen here. Have a good night." Flynn took a step back and closed the door, locking it before he was forced to deal with Brad's crazy ex for another second. As much as he'd enjoyed calling in a favor with one of his clients to get that surveillance footage sent to channel twelve, he wasn't much for drama. It was enough for him to know he'd helped out a friend, even if they never knew what he'd done. Flynn knew. That was enough.

"Did you just close the door in my brother's face?"

Flynn's head snapped around. A man with light brown hair and green eyes that matched Easton's sat quietly behind the front desk. Flynn had no idea how long he'd been sitting there. He could've been there since before Flynn slipped away from the party. Flynn had been too engrossed in the quiet to notice.

"I don't know. Is your brother a little blond guy who's stalking his ex?"

The gorgeous green gaze skirted away. He didn't have his brother's rage or glint of cruelty. Mostly, he looked tired. He stood. "I'll leave you to your thoughts." His white dress shirt looked fine and expensive, but the way he'd rolled his sleeves up to his elbows gave him a hint of approachability his younger brother didn't possess.

"There's enough space for two people to enjoy the silence here. I don't much care for crowds or noise," Flynn admitted.

A woeful green stare held his. "I'm Jake."

"Flynn. Can I get you another glass of champagne, Jake?" He purposefully said Jake's name to test it on his tongue.

"I should get back to the party."

Returning to the party wasn't what Jake really wanted. Flynn could hear the reluctance in his tone, but—for whatever reason—he felt he had to attend. Flynn didn't like being disobeyed.

"Let me rephrase my question. You'll have another glass of champagne. With me," he added, ensuring there would be no misunderstanding.

Jake's cool expression never wavered, but his eyes gave away his relief. He didn't like making decisions. They always felt wrong. Flynn knew people. He understood this one. "Okay."

The night looked brighter and brighter by the second. There was nothing Flynn enjoyed more than an obedient playmate with an ounce of fire. This one wouldn't bend easily. Flynn couldn't wait to see exactly how far Jake would let Flynn push him. Yep. Things were looking up.

Keep an eye out for the next Sugar Daddies book, *Sugar Alpha*.

PLEASE CONSIDER LEAVING a review at the retailer where this book was purchased. Reviews really help with a book's visibility, which ensures I can continue writing. Thank you, Charity.

ABOUT THE AUTHOR

Charity Parkerson is an award winning and multi-published author with several companies. Born with no filter from her brain to her mouth, she decided to take this odd quirk and insert it in her characters.

*Eight-time Readers' Favorite Award Winner
    *2015 Passionate Plume Award Finalist
    *2013 Reviewers' Choice Award Winner
    *2012 ARRA Finalist for Favorite Paranormal Romance
    *Five-time winner of The Mistress of the Darkpath

Connect with her online:

--Join my street team: facebook.com/TeamCharityParkerson
    --Sign up for my newsletter: http://bit.ly/CharityNews
    --Website: charityparkerson.com

--Facebook:
facebook.com/authorCharityParkerson
facebook.com/TheMenofSin
--Twitter: twitter.com/CharityParkerso